TWISTED TRAILS
by
Orlando Rigoni

Paul Scott had come all the way from Oklahoma seeking Alonzo Finch, who was responsible for the death of one of Paul's twin brothers and the disappearance of the other under a cloud. His path led him to a Mormon settlement in Utah, where he was offered a job pitching hay by the man who ran the trading post; and that in turn led him to a saloon called the Lone Chance, where he finally cornered his quarry.

However, because Paul knew he would never learn all the answers to what had happened in the past without Finch's help, and also because he wanted Finch legally tried, he had to suppress his natural desire for vengeance and refuse the invitation to a shoot-out.

THE BOOK INN
1816 Andrews St.
Phone 445-3305
Across from Southgate Mall, Alexandria

TWISTED TRAILS

TWISTED TRAILS

by

ORLANDO RIGONI

MAGNUM BOOKS
NEW YORK

© *Copyright 1965, by Arcadia House*

DEDICATED TO MY WIFE

CAROLYN BELLE

**PLAYMORE, INC., PUBLISHERS
and WALDMAN PUBLISHING CORP.
New York, New York**

Printed in the United States of America

TWISTED TRAILS

Chapter 1

Paul Scott urged his mount up the slant of West Dip, his warped hat tilted against the raw light of the high Utah country. The sun was a torment to be endured, just like the dust, the distance, and the chill, lonely nights.

At the top of the long climb, he pulled his horse to a stop, and his eyes embraced the bowl of the green valley below. A grunt of approval passed his lips. There were vivid green fields near the foot of the pass, and the raw scars of mines stabbing into the mountains that towered over them. Far to the east, he saw the dust and the confusion of a construction crew laying steel rails across the floor of the valley. He saw a trading post and what appeared to be a hotel about half a mile apart, and south of the fields was the stockade of an army post.

Scott dismounted, stretched his long legs and let his weary horse nibble at the scraggy bunch-grass.

He took off his warped hat and mopped his forehead with the sleeve of his shirt. In the narrow, wingless chaps, his legs looked like stovepipes.

"Mormons," he grunted. "If only Finch is there." His face was grim, and the shame he had suffered rose to the surface, raw and ragged. He pulled a sack of makings from his corduroy vest and, fashioning a smoke, clamped it in his lean jaw. He was a tall man, big-boned, with the meat slabbed on sparingly.

He thought back to the source of his bitterness. Alonzo Finch was the core of it. Scott couldn't absolve his twin brothers from all blame, for they had fallen easy prey to Finch's sly manner. Now Pete, one of the twins, was dead and Larry, the other, had sneaked away in shame, leaving that shame to be borne by the family. Where was Larry, he wondered; rotting dead and forsaken in some hidden gulch?

After a moment of reflection he mounted, riding down the slant that twisted and turned between sprawling hills. His eyes puckered. If these were Mormons, their confidence would be hard to gain. However, it was doubtful they would protect and harbor a man like Finch.

Paul's horse, scenting the lush alfalfa and the promise of water, trotted impatiently, his hooves spurting dust as they spurned the road. Suddenly the horse's head arched high, his ears at the alert. Rounding a sharp turn, Paul jerked his horse to a

TWISTED TRAILS 11

stop under the brow of a cutbank and stared at the scene ahead.

Two troopers, evidently drunk, had waylaid an old man and were badgering him unmercifully. The troopers had dismounted, and one of them grabbed the old man's beard, pulling him from the saddle of his rearing horse. The old man clawed and cussed but he was no match for the troopers. He fell to his knees and got an arm twisted around one of the trooper's legs.

The tall trooper with a lantern jaw snarled, "Frisk him, Miles. The mountain rat is bound to have gold on him!"

"Git him off my leg," Miles panted, kicking to free himself from the oldster's arms.

Lantern Jaw took two steps and gave the old man a vicious kick in the ribs that broke his hold and rolled him to the side of the trail. The oldster groaned and clutched his side.

"Darn it, Stebbins," the short, stocky man yelled, "don't kill him."

"Why not?" Stebbins grinned evilly. "He's gold mining, ain't he? He's got gold on him, or hid out some place. If he'll tell us, we'll split with him. If he won't—"

"You'd take it all an' kill me to boot," the old man panted.

Stebbins reached for a rock and hurled it at the

old man's horse, driving it away.

"Leastways, he'll have a long walk into Camp Boyd."

"Look out, Steb!" Milics warned.

The old man had fished a gun from somewhere inside his baggy coat and was rising to his knees. Stebbins whirled; the short whip in his gloved hand coiled and snapped around the oldster's wrist. A twisting pull, and the gun fell. A red bracelet of blood circled the old man's wrist and dripped like rubies across his knuckles.

Paul Scott, in the shadow of the bank, felt hate bitter in his mouth. He dug the spurs deep, and his horse cleared the intervening space in two bounds. Stebbins was reaching down for the gun when Paul landed on his back. Stebbins looked back, startled, and Paul smelled the reek of whiskey.

"Get off me!" Stebbins snarled, twisting to free himself. His surprise at finding a stranger attacking him was evident.

Paul spun him around and smashed his fist into the lantern jaw. Paul had strength, arms longer than average, but he was unschooled in the dog-eat-dog kind of fighting. Stebbins fell backward, and Paul, unbalanced by his impetuous attack, dropped to his knees. Stebbins doubled up his legs and kicked at Paul's chest, spurs, boots and all. Paul felt the air knocked from his lungs, felt the hot scorch of steel

TWISTED TRAILS 13

across his ribs. He rolled away, gasping, and staggered erect just as Miles circled to enter the fight.

It was too late to think of odds. Scott had cut himself into the fight, and he had to beat his way out or take a beating himself. He circled warily.

"Let's take him!" Stebbins barked, his long-jawed face as cunning as a wolf's.

The two men rushed from opposite sides. Scott twisted around and struck backward with his Mexican-roweled spurs. Miles, behind him, let out a yowl of pain. Scott swung all the way from his knee, and his fist exploded on Stebbin's lantern jaw.

"I'll take care o' this buzzard!" the old prospector said in a wheezy voice, straddling Stebbins' chest.

Paul had no time to answer. A blow on the back of his head sent him reeling. He kept his feet, turned and caught Miles coming at him. He crowded the shorter man, slamming punches at his head until Miles wilted. Scott beat him to his knees. While Miles whimpered, trying to protect his bloody face, Scott yanked him to his feet and struck him again. Miles fell, dazed.

Scott brushed his hair back and sucked the blood off his lip. He turned to see Stebbins roll over and pin the old man down. Stebbins jerked the old man's head up by his beard and was about to smash it against the hard trail.

"Turn him loose!" Paul cried.

Stebbins crouched to his feet, sobered. His floundering attack became careful, circling. He talked out of the corner of his mouth.

"Get up, Miles. Let's fix this boy!"

Scott, sucking air, followed Stebbins, who was feinting, biding his time. He was waiting for Miles to get up.

"Okay, Steb, okay," Miles panted. He stumbled forward.

Scott lunged and hit Stebbins in the stomach, slashed a blow across his face. Stebbins went down. Miles was pounding ineffectually on Scott's back. Scott turned and struck. Miles folded up and lay still. Stebbins stirred, mumbled something but did not rise.

"Danged lucky it's not you down there. They'd boot you in the head an' gouge your eyes out," the old man said, his teeth set against the pain in his side.

"Can you ride?" Scott asked, breathing hard. He watched the oldster's face with concern.

"Reckon I can, pardner."

"I'll get your horse," Scott said. He felt empty, beat up. Why did he have to get mixed up in trouble even before he reached the settlement?

"Be you goin' to leave 'em here like this?" the old man asked.

TWISTED TRAILS 15

"Why not? It might teach them a lesson." Scott smiled crookedly. Then he had another thought. He rode over to the troopers' mounts and, hooking the reins over the saddles, started them toward the post.

"They won't like that," the old man said.

"Give them a dose of their own medicine. They were putting you afoot," Scott said, and rode over to catch the straying horse.

Together they rode down the slant toward Camp Boyd. The picture came into sharper focus as they neared the settlement. Men could be seen milling about the army post. Stragglers came to and went from the hotel. It was curious how in all that vast land, people had chosen that spot in which to live. It was cut off from the world. But the lure of gold, the miracle of water had attracted them and cemented them together.

Scott looked at the old man and saw his face set and twisted with pain he would not acknowledge. He saw Scott's glance and forced a grin.

"Aaron Sodek—that's me—" he said, "is mighty grateful, son. He won't forget what you done."

"Paul Scott here," he replied. He pulled his ear. "I'm a mite curious."

"Yeah? 'Bout what?"

"Do you have any gold?"

Sodek grimaced. "Cain't rightly say. Mebbe I do, an' mebbe I don't."

"All right; keep it to yourself. I'm not looking for gold."

"Uriah Young," Aaron said, "has been grubstakin' me fer years. He owns the trading post yonder. He's sort of bishop of the church around here for what Mormons there are."

"Those troopers must have had some hunch you had gold. They were laying for you."

"Pure chance, son. I been out in the hills. There is gold there; it's been proven. Them boys was likkered up. They put two and two together and figured to badger me. If they was sober, they would never have tried to rob me, not with Major Hornaby commanding the post."

"What's the post doing here?" Paul asked. "A marshal could enforce what law there is."

The older man frowned. "The post is a hangover from when the federal troops came out to break up polygamy. There are some Indians here, and they need watching. Then the gold strike is bringing in a rough element."

Sodek's horse stumbled, and the old man clutched his side while his face winced with pain. Scott felt his anger against the troopers rise.

"It couldn't be any rougher than the troopers."

"It's a rough country. What are you doin' here, Scott? Driftin'? Come to stay?"

"I'm looking for a man."

"Name him," Sodek said shortly.

"Finch—Alonzo Finch. Heard of him?"

"Cain't say. Been gone for a spell. You might ask Uriah—he runs the trading post. Most honest men stop there."

"And the dishonest men?"

"Ask Addie or Lieth Severs at the Lone Chance about 'em. Your man might be there now; he might come. You got livin' money?"

"Some. I had a long chase."

"Uriah might put you up. He could use a hand. Better come with me an' see him. Fact is, I do have some gold, but it ain't rightly mine. It's Uriah's."

"You mean you find gold for Uriah? Why not stake it for yourself?"

"Uriah pays the tithes out of it, an' the rest—well, it ain't a story to tell strangers," Sodek finished in a husky voice.

When Paul met Uriah Young in the gloom of the trading post, he felt an instant liking for the man. His reddish whiskers were trimmed to match those of Brigham Young himself, and Paul wondered if there was any relationship between Uriah and the Mormon leader. Uriah's thick arms and beefy shoulders made light work of moving the sacks of grain. At first he was on the defensive.

"Hello. Brother Aaron. Have you found another

fool trying to wheedle your claim from you?"

"Hold on there, Uriah. This is Paul Scott. Mind if I set a spell? I don't feel right good," Aaron said, holding his side and sitting down slowly on a sack of grain.

Uriah turned and gave Paul's cut and blood-smeared face a searching look. "Why didn't you send him to Addie's?"

"He did me a favor, Brother Uriah. I was ambushed on the trail by a couple of troopers. They was mean. I got my side caved in to prove it. Scott beat them off me, as you can see by his face. Thought you might put him up."

"Trail tramps won't work. They don't stay long enough to get used to the water."

Paul extended his hand. "Right proud to know you, sir," he said, ignoring Uriah's words.

Taking Paul's hand, Uriah said, "Where you from?"

"Oklahoma. My folks have a store and ranch there, something like this. We run some cattle."

"I could use a hand," Uriah conceded.

"I'm not a Mormon."

"Have I asked that? I need somebody who ain't too proud to haul hay. I can get riders, or freight haulers, but pitching hay is beneath them. Lazy, Mormon or gentile. I've got a contract to haul a load of hay a day to the army post. I could use the hay my-

TWISTED TRAILS

self, but if I don't sell it to them, they'll take it anyway. If you could just haul me that one load of hay and maybe help unload the freight when it comes in—"

"Reckon I won't be here long enough for that, sir."

"What's the matter with this place? It's the best valley between here and Saint George. You should have been here twelve years ago when they moved everybody down from Salt Lake the time the federal troops come out. We had a camp then. Took care of thirty thousand, mostly plural wives and their kids. Still got marks of them here, an junk they left behind. You could pick a worse place to settle, son."

"I'm looking for a man—Alonzo Fitch. Know him?"

Uriah's sharp eyes puckered, and he brushed his thinning hair across his head with his clawed fingers.

"Can't say I know him, but that don't mean he ain't here. I don't cotton none to the deadfall up the road. It's a sinful place, but I leave the devil to look after his own. Addie keeps her men and girls in line. Finch could be there."

"Then I won't bother you any more," Paul Scott said.

"Why such a hurry?" a soft voice asked from the shadows behind the front door.

Paul frowned. It had been a long time since he had heard the voice of a woman, and this voice disturbed him. He searched the shadows and saw the white oval of her face. It appeared to float there, disembodied.

"I'm not hurrying. It's a planned thing," Paul said.

She moved toward him, slow, graceful and beautiful.

"You were asked to dinner," she said, looking up at him. There was rebuke in her brown eyes. "Is it polite to refuse?"

"I wasn't asked," Paul objected, feeling uncomfortable at the sudden appearance of this poised girl. "Your friend here, Brother Aaron, begged for me because he felt he owed me something."

"Then I'm asking you," she said gravely.

Uriah broke in. "Why have you come here, Norah?"

"You never asked me that before, Father. I come when I please. Who is this man?"

Aaron Sodek squirmed on the sack of grain, and a groan escaped him. "He's Paul Scott," Aaron said through set teeth. "Not a man to have his nose ringed, Norah, even by you."

"Do you mean he's a tramp?" the girl asked, looking sideways at Scott.

"Pay her no mind," Uriah Young said. "She ain't been broke to the bit yet. If you won't stay, you won't stay. I hoped you was a man who wouldn't shy from sweat and blisters. If you change your mind—"

"I'm right grateful, sir. Now if you'll excuse me—" Paul turned toward the door, keeping his eyes from

Norah with an effort.

"My, but we're full of starch," Norah said. "Are you mad at me?"

Paul felt his own face redden. "Might be I'm touchy. No offense intended. And thanks for the invite."

He pushed out into the hot afternoon sun and stood for a moment getting his bearings. Off to the left, behind the store, flowed and frothed a miraculous spring. It gushed from the earth a stream full-born and babbled toward the broad green acres of Uriah Young a quarter of a mile distant. The ranch house, what he could see of it, looked lost and dwarfed among the giant cottonwoods. A half-mile down the valley, and connected to the spring with a wooden flume, stood the military post.

He turned, mounted his horse and rode toward the two-story frame building some distance up the road toward the mines. Near the building sprawled the shacks and office of the contractor building the railroad. It was a fabulous railroad, crawling straight as a die across the flats and then zigzagging up the face of the mountain in a series of switchbacks. There were tents there, too, in which the tracks crews slept when they were glutted with working, drinking, gambling and brawling.

A skinny old man with a tobacco-stained beard untangled his long legs on the steps of the porch.

"Howdy, stranger," the man said. He weaved unsteadily.

"Howdy. Do they stable horses here? Mine's tired an' hungry."

"Come far?" the man prodded.

Paul didn't like nosy strangers. "Far enough."

"There's a corral out back. Hay's in the shed. I'll take care of him if you want."

Paul reconsidered. His stay there might be short. Finch might have come and gone. He might not have arrived. In either case there would be sense in him spending money waiting at the Lone Chance.

"Never mind," he told the skinny man, who immediately tangled himself up again on the step.

After tying his horse at the rail, Paul entered the building.

The stale smell of liquor met him as he blinked against the dim light. His eyes took in the interior, the long pine bar, the tables near the door, the dance floor beyond and the stairs leading upward into dark, secret places. With the same glance he saw the tableau at the table to his left. A miner stood crouched over his kicked back chair, a gun in his hand. The man at the side of the table backed toward the bar, his eyes staring fascinated at the gun. Across the table, his hands clawed motionless above some cards, his handsome face exuding sweat and a smile still on his lips, although the mirth had gone out of it, sat

TWISTED TRAILS

Alonzo Finch!

As Paul stood momentarily poised, the words, "You cheatin' tinhorn!" seemed still to hang in the air—hang over Alonzo Finch as his eyes stared at death. The miner's was no idle threat. Even Paul understood that, and realized the man had drawn for one purpose only. Paul knew, too, that Alonzo Finch must not die. If he did, the journey of twelve-hundred miles would have been for nothing.

With the step of a cat, Paul moved behind the crouched miner. He heard a commotion on the stairs but dared not turn his head. Once before today he had blundered into trouble, double trouble. He gave no thought to odds, or who might back the miner up. He knew only that Alonzo Finch must not die. Lifting his booted foot, Paul stiff-legged against the hinge of the miner's knee. The unexpected action buckled the man's leg, and he pivoted, crashing back across the upset chair. Cursing, the man threw his right hand down to catch himself. Paul placed his boot across the thick brown wrist and pressed. The gun slid free, and with a quick motion Paul kicked it across the floor.

The miner rolled free of the chair and crouched to his thick legs, roaring and weaving like a wounded bear. Instinctively, Paul moved back against the wall, expecting the attack. The attack never came. A woman's voice, a firm, throaty voice, said from the bottom of the stairs:

"Morgan, pick up your money and go home!"

The miner, consumed with fury at the man who had cheated him of money and the man who had cheated him of revenge, closed his big-knuckled hands, hands used to swinging a sixteen-pound double-jack all day, upon the back of the broken chair. With one motion he swung the wreck high and brought it crashing down upon Finch's back. Then his fury died and he looked about him with bloodshot eyes.

"Take up your money, Morgan, and get," the woman said in a quieter voice.

Paul saw her then, draped in a dress of white. Not a jewel marred the simplicity of her costume, or the taffy-colored hair swept upward in a pompadour. The woman wore her years secretly, as though she had been cast from a mold complete and endowed. Even without the skillfully applied make-up, her skin would have been soft and without flaw. And yet all the overripe loveliness was but a showcase for the nerveless, determined, commanding presence underneath.

"I'm sorry, Addie," the miner grumbled.

"Come back when you can behave, Morgan," Addie said.

"I didn't know you harbored cheats, Addie; my mistake."

"I give every man one chance," Addie said. "Mr.

TWISTED TRAILS

Finch has had his."

Alonzo Finch had straightened in his chair and shoved his hat forward to the usual jaunty angle. The moisture had seeped back into his wide, flat-planed face, and his smile thawed to one of ironical humor.

Oddly enough, the cards were still in order upon the green-topped table. A stud hand, with one card face down. Before Finch lay a ten, jack, queen and king of hearts. Before Morgan's place lay a pair of treys, a four, a king—and he had turned up another king. Finch hadn't yet turned up his card. He did so now with a negligent flip of his long-boned hand. It was a six!

"It's your money, Morgan," Finch said casually; "pick it up."

Paul found himself admiring Alonzo's adroitness. By a move of his hand and a few words, he had put them in the position of owing him an apology.

Somewhat sheepishly, Morgan picked up the money and went out. Before the door closed, Paul found his eyes clashing with Finch's gray eyes.

"What are you doing here, Paul?" Finch asked.

Paul was conscious of Addie watching them.

"Do you have to ask that, Alonzo?" Paul countered.

"This is a big country, Paul. A man of your talents should do well here, but there's one funny thing about all this space. If a man wants trouble, he can find it without half trying. Be smart and ride on."

Paul read the threat in Finch's words. Shaking his head slowly, he said, "This is as far as I go. You left a trail as crooked as your own crooked heart. Now you're going back to Oklahoma with me to face the music."

Finch said in the same unhurried voice, "You better be careful, Paul. If you keep makin' them long speeches in this high altitude, you'll run out of wind. Suppose I don't want to go, you going to tie me up and pack me on your back?"

"I'll find a way to get you back," Paul replied.

"I won't be much good to you dead."

"That I know. Why do you think I horned into your fight?"

"I forgot to thank you for that, Paul," Finch acknowledged. "You got a warrant for me? This is Utah territory."

"Before I get through, you'll be glad to go back, Alonzo."

"Paul," Alonzo said, rising and walking toward the stairs, "you're going to spring a hole in your head with all those big ideas. Remember what I told you about the altitude?"

At the foot of the stairs, Alonzo turned toward Addie. "When do you expect Lieth back, ma'am?"

"A week, maybe," Addie answered, her eyes on Paul.

"Thank you," Finch said with elaborate politeness, and walked away into the darkness. Then Paul heard Addie's warm, throaty voice. She was moving toward the bar with a gliding motion, as though she were mounted on wheels.

"Come over here, stranger," she said. "I'll buy you a drink."

Paul went to the bar, and the barkeep heaved his fat body erect and waddled toward them. The other card player had disappeared during the excitement.

"Whiskey," Paul said, his eyes meeting Addie's. "The name's Paul Scott."

"I saw you handle that miner, and I liked what I saw," Addie said as they raised their glasses. She sipped hers and set it down.

"Thank you," said Paul.

"What was your trouble with Alonzo Finch?"

"It has nothing to do with this country or you, ma'am."

"Call me Addie; everybody does. I didn't mean to stick my long nose into your business," Addie said, giving him a quick smile.

"Your nose isn't long," he replied. "When did Finch get here?"

"He's been here a month. I haven't got him figured out yet, and I'm pretty good at figuring. He already seems to have some kind of hold on Lieth Severs, my partner."

"That's how he works. Where is your partner? Are you running this place alone?"

"I am right now. Lieth's gone to Salt Lake on some land business. They've been re-surveying some of this country since the railroad and mines came. I need a man here. I thought I had one in Lieth." Her voice dropped, and a shadow of sadness crossed her eyes.

"You are in love with him?"

"How can one love something that's not whole?" she asked softly. "I need a man who can handle himself to help me take care of things here. It's quiet at this time of day, but later, when the men knock off work, they'll swarm in here. They're a mixed bunch. I think you're the man for the job."

"I'm sorry, ma'am. . . ."

"Call me Addie," she prompted again.

"I'm right sorry, Addie, but I can't work for you. I'm going to be here just long enough to get Alonzo Finch out of camp. What good could I do you in that length of time?"

"Have you figured a way to get him out?"

"I will."

"There's only one way I see, and it will take time. You'd have to keep it quiet, though, so that he could not escape you. Send a message with the stage tomorrow to send over the telegraph from Salt Lake to Oklahoma. Have the sheriff there send a warrant to the U.S. marshal at Provo. He can come over, arrest

TWISTED TRAILS

Finch legally, and maybe deputize you to take him back."

There it was—the legal way, the right way.

"But that will take weeks," Paul objected.

"Two weeks maybe—three. How long have you been on Finch's trail?"

"Couple of months."

"Then why begrudge the time? While you're here, you can earn your keep. I'll guarantee you won't be bored," Addie promised.

Paul could feel the woman reining him hard, and he fought the bit stubbornly. In one afternoon he had confronted two women and had had two offers of jobs.

"I've already got a job," he surprised himself by saying.

"Miner? Laborer?"

"Uriah Young. He needs a man to haul hay."

"Oh, I saw you riding into camp with old Sodek. Have you met Norah?"

The inflection in the throaty voice irritated Paul.

"What has Norah got to do with it?"

"Don't jump down my throat, Paul. I didn't say she had anything to do with it. It just seems strange you should take a job with Uriah without a special reason. You're not a farmhand."

Paul was vaguely aware that they were quarreling, and it puzzled him.

"What do you think I am, Addie? A roustabout? A swamper? A gunnie to whip your customers into line?"

Addie laughed softly. "She's a beautiful girl, Paul. A good girl, but still a little wet behind the ears."

Outside, the first of the evening's customers was fogging dust toward the Lone Chance. Addie walked to the stairs without looking back, and Paul watched her go. At the foot of the stairs she turned.

"If you change your mind, Paul, let me know."

Without answering, he pushed through the door, and the miners, lathered with sweat and stained red from the blood of the earth, made way for him on the porch.

He mounted his horse and headed for the ranch.

Chapter 2

The next morning Norah, still abed, heard the loaded hayrack rattle and bounce across the rocky creek bottom on its way to the stockade. Cherry, an Indian girl who helped with the housework, always cooked early breakfast for the men. She had been taught the simple tasks of frying hogmeat, eggs and potatoes. Being Mormons, the Youngs drank no coffee. But there was plenty of milk, and for the more hardy, Brigham tea, brewed from a local bush. The more complicated cooking was done by Helen, Uriah's wife.

What had Paul done at Addie's? He had been there a long time, and something that had happened there had brought him back to the ranch to work for Uriah. Had he found Alonzo Finch? If he had, there would be little reason for him remaining there. No, it must have been something to do with Addie. He was staying so that he could see Addie again. The thought made her uncomfortable. If it was Addie who was keeping him there, why didn't he stay at the Lone Chance?

Norah arose and dressed leisurely before she raised the blind. The sun rushed into the room, spreading a golden rug upon the carpet. Norah surveyed herself in her mirror and frowned at the brown and gold picture she made. Why should she not go up to Addie's and ask her about Paul?

But she wouldn't go to Addie's dressed in boots and buckskin and flannel. She would show Addie she could be a lady, too. Pulling the blind down again, she took off her riding clothes and put on a starched gingham dress, white and blue, with a small red bow at the throat. She pulled on black stockings and forced her feet into small pointed-toe shoes that always pinched before an hour had passed. Unraveling her thick braids, she combed out her hair and drew it up in a roll on the top of her head.

She turned as the door opened and saw the shocked expression on her mother's face.

"What are you doing in those clothes at this time of day?" Helen asked sharply.

Norah pleaded, "Let's not quarrel again, Mother."

"Quarrel, indeed! Is it quarreling to ask what you're up to? You should have had your breakfast long ago. It's after nine o'clock."

"I'll get my own breakfast."

"But those clothes. If you're doing it for the new man Uriah put to work, it will do you no good. He's been gone for some time with a load of hay for the post. Besides, what have I told you about mixing with the help?"

"Don't worry; I'm not going to make a fool of myself."

"Then why the starch and ribbons at this hour?"

"I'm going up to Addie's."

"Up to Addie's? Are you out of your mind?" Helen gasped.

"I've been there before."

"Do you know what you're saying? How many times have you been there? Why haven't I heard of it?"

"It was over a year ago, Mother, the time she had the singer from Salt Lake. She let me sit in the dining room and listen. It was wonderful."

"Indeed! If you put some paint on your lips and some powder on your face, perhaps she'll give you a job!"

"I have no paint or powder. I wish I had."

"Do you want to disgrace us all, Norah? If you want to flirt with Mr. Scott, do it here at home where he can't take advantage of you," Helen said.

"Mother, don't be so naïve. I'm grown up. . . ."

"This is what comes of being born and reared in this wild, uncouth land. You don't know the value of things, the worth of people. How could you?"

"Look, Mother, I spent three years finishing my schooling in Salt Lake. Of course that's not New York, or even Denver, but there are civilized people there."

"You should have found a husband, then," Helen said.

"I didn't go there to find a husband. Is that how you met Uriah?"

"Your father was different. When he came to St. Louis with a shipment of furs, he was a wild, romantic figure. I guess I lost my head," Helen said reminiscently.

"Do you regret it?"

"I don't regret loving Uriah, but I do regret having had to give up so much. I thought some day I could take you back where people are civilized. . . ."

"But I like my life here!" Norah interposed. "This is my home."

"And don't let Mr. Scott get a hold on you," Helen said. "Soon he'll be gone, and you'll suffer. I know. Look, there's Major Hornaby. He'll be transferred east soon. You could do worse."

"We've discussed Major Hornaby before, Mother. Now I must go."

"You're not changing your clothes, then? How will you get to the Lone Chance? Will you walk in those shoes?"

TWISTED TRAILS

"I'll have Egg harness up the buggy," she said, using the nickname of a hand named Eglund.

"So we're going to be a lady, are we?" her mother jibed. "Well, remember what I told you." She went out, closing the door not too gently.

Once on the road, Norah felt conspicuous and a little less sure of herself.

But by the time she reached the Lone Chance, she had regained her composure. The sun, beating against the red front of the big building, cast a rosy reflection in the dust. She was about to alight from the carriage to tie her horse at the long rail when a man descended with a firm yet jaunty step from the shadows of the veranda. Norah paused in the act of alighting to stare at him.

She was unaware of having seen the man before, yet he bore a resemblance to someone she knew. For the moment she was unable to say who, because she was too absorbed in the man himself. His boots gleamed in the sun, and his creased trousers were pulled down over them. He wore no coat, but his broad shoulders were covered with a flannel shirt that flaunted a yellow string tie. She could almost smell the pomade that shone on the dark hair framing a wide, flat-planed face.

The voice that spoke to her was soft and courteous.

"May I have the pleasure of offering you my services, Miss Young?"

The sound of her name on the stranger's lips surprised her. Dubiously, she replied, "I can do for myself."

"No harm intended, Miss Young. Here; let me help you down."

His hand was soft, but impersonal, and Norah attempted to be gracious.

"Thank you, sir."

"Here, let me tie your horse for you."

"Thank you," she repeated, then tried to keep from running to the entrance of the dining room.

When she entered the dining room, with its smell of scrubbed floors and food being cooked for the noon-day meal, she was still perturbed by the incident outside. The startled look on the face of the girl setting out clean dishes upon the long tables annoyed her.

"Will you tell Addie I'd like to speak with her, Jen?" she said, keeping her voice steady.

"Why—why, certainly, ma'am—I mean, Norah—say, what's this all about?" Jen looked puzzled. "You gettin' married?"

"No, Jen. Tell Addie I want to talk with her."

Jen disappeared, shaking her head from side to side. Norah remained standing, feeling out of place. She heard Addie say something in the barroom through the open door. The next minute Addie appeared.

"You want to speak to me?" she asked, her eyes curious under their dark lashes.

"I wanted to talk to you. Of course I know you're not to blame, but you could be helpful if you wanted to," Norah said evasively.

"What are you talking about, Norah?" Addie asked suspiciously.

"I'm talking about Egg."

"Yes? What about Eglund?"

"He doesn't take care of his job. He comes up here to drink and play cards when he should be working," Norah said quickly.

"And you dressed in your best bib and tucker to come and tell me about it?"

"You're dressed up, aren't you?" Norah defended herself.

"It's my business to be dressed up. I wouldn't look quite so appealing as you in buckskin and flannel. Now tell me what this is all about?"

"My father, he thinks Egg's working. . . ."

"All right, Norah, you've made your excuse for coming. Let's sit down. Now tell me just why you came? Did you expect to find Paul here?"

Norah felt a flush warm her face, and it angered her. "All right, Addie," she said, her chin up. "I came to find out what happened here yesterday."

"Don't be evasive, Norah," Addie said. "That other

time you were here, I told you to go home and grow up. Well, don't overdo it."

Norah had her gloves off, and now she creased them upon the end of the table.

"When Paul came in to dinner last night, he met Egg. I could tell that he had seen Egg before, and this is the only place he could have seen him. Now tell me what happened," Norah pleaded.

"There was a fight over a card game," Addie admitted, and went on to tell in detail just what had happened, emphasizing Paul's part in the argument, but not mentioning any other names.

Norah's eyes were alight. She felt an inner glow of satisfaction.

"He's brave, isn't he?"

"He's brave and quick. Good qualities in a man."

"Maybe he's a lawman in disguise, looking for someone," Norah suggested.

Addie shook her head. "I don't think so. I offered him a job, and he wouldn't take it."

"So you did try to hold him," Norah charged.

Addie, impatient, said, "I only offered him a job. If he's going to hang around here, he might as well earn his keep."

"And how would he earn his keep, Addie—by being nice to you?" Norah was sorry for the remark as soon as she said it.

"Norah, stop talking like that; it doesn't become

you," Addie said almost in a motherly tone. "I'm sure Paul is a man to pick his own woman. He won't be picking her around here, because he won't be here long enough."

"How do you know? Did he tell you?"

"Yes, he did. He came looking for a man. It's a grudge fight, a feud, a vendetta. Do you know what that is, Norah? It's something to stay away from, because it curdles people, makes them hard and dangerous. Don't lose your head over Paul, Norah. Soon he'll be gone."

"But until he finds his man—"

"He has found him."

"You mean Alonzo Finch is here?"

There was no need for Addie to reply. A voice from the barroom did it for her.

"Did somebody call my name?" Finch said, smiling at the two women, his flat-crowned hat in his hands.

Norah looked up and for a moment sat immobile. There stood the man with the fancy clothes, the shiny hair, the inquisitive penetrating eyes whom she had met outside. This was the man Paul was after. Rising hastily, she turned to the door and almost ran from the room.

"Thanks, Addie," she said over her shoulder, not sure for what she was thanking the woman.

Alonzo Finch saw the girl's panic, and it amused

him.

In her haste, Norah had left her gloves, and now Addie reached for them. Alonzo Finch's long, soft hand moved snake-like and fingered them away from her.

"These are mine to return, Addie," he said. "That's the prerogative of a gentleman."

"Norah isn't a woman, Alonzo; she's just an inexperienced girl."

"Why not let me find that out for myself, Addie?"

Finch knew he was exasperating Addie, and it gave him pleasure.

"You think you know where Lieth Severs has gone, don't you?" he prodded her further.

"He's gone to Salt Lake to check up on the new land surveys, same as Hebe Farrow did for the mine and Carmody for the railroad."

"I told him to tell you that, Addie. It would give you something logical to think about."

"Then where is he?"

"He's where I sent him. You see, Addie, all people have past lives, and some of them are very dangerous."

"You're lying—you're trying to frighten me," Addie charged.

"Why should I try to frighten you? If Lieth comes back like we agreed, then I'll leave this place. It's that simple."

TWISTED TRAILS

He saw Addie pulling herself together.

"On the contrary, Alonzo," she said, "I intend to warn the girl about you."

"Oh, come now, Addie. Wouldn't that be absurd? It would be the pot calling the kettle black. I'm not an ignorant blackguard. I have charm and personality. I'm sure I have the knowledge and the manners to impress her," he said, stuffing the gloves into the pocket of his tight-fitting pants.

Paul Scott, his long body cradled in the load of hay, watched the rhythmic rumps of the sleek horses below him as he drove the team down the dusty road. The nest of alfalfa was fragrant and sweet.

He clucked to the horses and focused his eyes on the circular outlines of the fort, which was nothing more than a stockade, a boundary to separate the military from the rest of the world. The stockade was constructed of a warp of cedar poles, their butts thrust into the earth, with a weft of heavy wire binding them together. The Indians were quiet now, and the Mormons offered no further physical resistance to federal authority, so this outpost was but a symbol of power, keeping the peace more by its presence than by its authority.

As Paul drove up to the heavy, counterbalanced gate, it swung open grudgingly on its tallowed hinges, and Sergeant McCune was inside to welcome him.

Paul, following the sergeant's waving arms, pulled the wagon upon the big scales and kicked the brake tight before sliding to the ground.

The short, thick sergeant thrust out his hand, and Paul winced at the pressure of it. A smile of welcome wreathed the sergeant's red, weathered face.

"McCune's the name," the sergeant said. "I see you're another one."

"Paul Scott here," Paul said, and added, "What did you mean by that last remark, Sergeant?"

"Uriah has a tough time gettin' the fodder delivered. Sometimes he brings it himself. Sometimes he sends Eglund, but Eglund doesn't like to come. Looks to me like he's scared of this place. Even Norah has delivered the hay in a pinch." McCune laughed.

Paul felt rebuked. "Looks like I took a woman's job, then."

"Now don't be touchy, Scott. That girl can tackle anything and still be a lady. Come to my quarters while the men unload the hay. They're busy right now; it'll take a little time."

Paul followed the stocky, cocksure man toward the row of huts that disected the stockade. McCune led the way into an orderly room, cramped but spotless. The earth floor had been dampened and swept until its hardened surface was like tile. Along one wall a shelf held books which intrigued Paul. They were mostly classics, but there were books on law and

TWISTED TRAILS 43

medicine.

Digging into the straw of his neatly made-up bunk, McCune drew forth a bottle of whiskey. Holding the bottle behind him, he stuck his bristly head out the door and looked carefully around. Then he closed the door.

"The major's death against liquor on the post. He has issued a written order, posted on the bulletin board, that liquor is prohibited on the post under penalty of imprisonment. Here, have a drink."

Paul accepted the drink in the spirit in which it was offered.

"How did you happen to arrive at this place, McCune?" Paul asked. "There's not much future in it, is there?"

McCune smacked his lips over the strong liquor and put the bottle back in his bunk.

"Let me tell you, lad," he replied: "today is yesterday's future. Beyond that a man can't tell. The future, the present and the past are all in every tick of the clock. A man can't put his finger on any of them. I went to California when the gold fever was on. I was young and tough enough to hold my own. Staked a good claim near what later became Columbia on the Stanislaus River. Didn't take me long to learn that me an' money wouldn't get along very good. Too much firewater, too many fights, an' the gold siftin' through my calloused fingers. I woke up disgusted one day and saw I was a fool. I had a neighbor in camp with a wife an' two kids. How they had the gall to go there I don't know. This neighbor didn't have any luck, so I up an' gave him my claim.

Fiscoli was his name. He insisted I keep half the claim, but I told him it would only bring me grief. Fiscoli made good, bought land with his gold, and has a right nice place out there. They still write to me, an' I've got a home to go to when my soldierin' is done. That's more than I'd have if I'd kept the claim."

Paul said, "That makes sense, I guess. It don't explain why you're here, though."

"Army lad. I joined up durin' the war. Come under the major's command at the battle of Vicksburg." McCune added in a curiously plaintive voice, as though he were pleading for understanding, "He needs me—here I am."

Paul didn't know what to answer, so he suggested they see if the hay was unloaded.

Other freight wagons had come in with supplies from more distant places, their tall wheels grinding up the dust and fingering it into the air. The empty wagons lumbered about in the cramped space, heading out for open country.

"Watch this, now," McCune told Paul, grinning.

"Where?" Paul inquired.

"That wagon that just unloaded, the one with the driver with the brush on his face."

TWISTED TRAILS 45

Paul watched the indicated wagon. He saw the big end gate swinging open, stay chains dragging on the ground. The big hooks on the ends of the chains bobbed and bit at the earth. The wagon, making an awkward turn, lumbered over a pile of rope. The searching hook of the dragging chain on the left of the wagon reached for and snagged a full coil of rope.

"Once he got away with a bundle of shovels that way. I heard about it later, but it couldn't be proved, so I let it go. He's been trying ever since. Innocent as a babe, he drives on, hoping nobody will notice." McCune gave an infectious chuckle.

The big wagon lumbered on through the gate, but suddenly the sentry shouted at the driver to stop, which he did. McCune barked at two men to go over and unhook the coil of rope from the chain, and while they did so, the bearded face of the freight hauler looked back ruefully.

There was a general shouting back and forth of good-natured insults, as the driver accused them of robbing him.

"When a man catches a fish on his hook, no man has a right to take it off!" the driver declared.

The commotion could be heard all across the stockade, and it brought Major Hornaby to the door of his office. Picking up his wide-brimmed hat, he placed it on his head in precisely the right manner and marched across the compound. The sun flashed from the polished leather of his boots and belt. The creases in his trousers were knife-sharp. The expression on his long, aristocratic face was stern and uncompromising. His face was sharp-boned, but well proportioned, and he had that indefinable quality of a man of breeding.

Sergeant McCune saluted the major perfunctorily, a salute which the major put to shame with one of his own.

"What seems to be the trouble here, Sergeant?"

"Ownby, the old coot from Provo, snagged a coil of rope with his gate chain. We took it away from him."

Paul saw the skin on the major's cheekbones tighten.

"You will address me as 'sir,' Sergeant, when strangers are present," the major said tartly.

"Ownby, the old coot from Provo, snagged a coil of rope with his end gate chain, *sir*." McCune recited the complete statement like a ritual.

Paul saw annoyance sharpen the major's features.

"All these civilians are crooks," Hornaby charged. "They believe the army is here to be preyed upon. If we didn't watch them every minute, we'd starve on our appropriations."

"Quite so, *sir*," McCune echoed dutifully.

Hornaby turned to McCune and said testily, "Oh, be still Sergeant. I don't know whether you are trying to make an ass of yourself or of me."

"Sorry, *sir*."

Hornaby ignored this and asked, "Did you sign for the hay, Sergeant?"

McCune thrust the paper at him, and though his face was immobile and his bearing stiff, there was a warm salute in his eyes. Paul climbed onto the rack and, standing with feet braced, urged the horses back through the gate and up the road.

In the ranch yard, he unhitched the team and drove them into the barn.

He took his time unharnessing. It was already past noon. Rather than ask Mrs. Young to set out dinner for him, he would go get something to eat at Addie's. After all, that would give him a chance to check on Alonzo. He grained the team and turned them out the back door of the barn into the adjoining pasture. Returning to the front door of the barn, which faced the house, he was surprised to see Alonzo Finch backing off the porch, doffing his hat and bowing.

Turning into the barn, he saddled his horse and, without pausing at the house, headed toward the Lone Chance.

The Lone Chance appeared to wait with eager expectancy for the day shift to get off work, as today was pay day. A few of the night shift men sat on the shady porch, drinking either on credit or borrowed cash. Paul dismounted slowly, keeping his eyes alert, his gun pulled around so he could reach it with the butt forward.

Inside the barroom at the bar he saw three or four strangers who turned and stared at him. "Bighead" Larson, the apelike man who swamped out the bar, was busy with a mop near the back of the room. His oversized head appeared to sit directly on his shoulders without a neck. He turned his body half around and looked questioningly at Paul.

"Have you seen Finch?" Paul asked.

The big, shaggy head shook in the negative. Then Addie appeared on the stairs and smiled at Paul.

"I saw you coming from the window," she said. "Now I hear you ask for Alonzo Finch. You didn't impress me as a troublesome man, Paul."

"Hello, Addie," he said, adding, "I'm the sort of man who learns a lesson and learns it good. Never let trouble get to you first. Go out and find it, if it's there."

"But it's such a small thing, Paul. It's not worth fighting about. He just went there to return her gloves," Addie said testily.

Paul stared at her, perplexed. "Her gloves? Whose gloves? What are you talking about?"

It was the first time he had seen Addie flush. She did so now because she had given herself away.

"Never mind," she said, regaining her composure. "Have you had your dinner?"

"No."

"Then perhaps you'll dine with me?"

Seated across from Addie, who was laced and ruffled, Paul felt out of place in his working clothes.

"Has Finch come here lately?" he asked as they ate the hot, nourishing food. The sweet smell of corned beef and cabbage and the pungent warmth of hot bread badgered his appetite.

"I didn't see him. But I want no trouble today, Paul. It's going to be a wild night. If you can't work for me and fight for me, then take your personal quarrels somewhere else."

"I'll start no fight here," Paul promised. Then he added, "What did you mean about the gloves?"

"Never mind," she told him.

They finished the meal in silence. Paul thanked her and strolled back into the bar. She did not look up as he left.

Finch was standing at the bar, in conversation with a couple of the miners and having a drink at their expense. Paul walked up casually, pushed in alongside Finch and ordered a brandy.

"Just got through eating," he volunteered. "Where you eating your meals these days, Finch?"

Finch half turned and smiled at him. "You're taking a very personal interest in my welfare, aren't you, Paul?"

"I'm trying to keep you good and healthy for the

trip home, Alonzo."

"I aim to stay healthy, and I feel very healthy here. Good climate. Quit stalling and have your say."

"What were you doing at the ranch last night?"

"Me? What would I be doing there?"

"I don't know. I'm just asking."

"Look, Paul; you don't have to act like a hay hauler just because you are one."

Paul felt the cords in his neck stiffen. Before he could retort, Alonzo turned around and said, "Are these troopers friends of yours, Paul? They appear to be taking your measure."

The two troopers he had fought the day before had come in unobtrusively. Stebbins, with his long jackass jaw, stood with his back to the door, and Miles was moving forward slowly but purposefully on his short, thick legs. The cut on his face from the battle of the day before had barely closed. Stebbins' left eye still had a discouraged hue.

Paul stood with his back against the bar, not moving.

"Howdy, men," Paul greeted them affably. "You gave me a tough go yesterday. How about a drink on it?"

He was making an overture of peace if they cared to accept it.

"Granted," Miles said, circling to the end of the bar, "we were out of line yesterday. We were rough on the old coot. But he could have saved himself the beating."

"How?"

"By answering our questions."

"He had no answers. There is no gold."

"There's some who think different. But no matter. A man resents a whipping. More than that, a trooper resents being sent home on foot. If you've got any guts, stand away from the bar!"

Paul could not watch both men at once. He kept his eye on Miles, and saw the savage expectancy in his beady eyes. "Let's take it outside, Miles," he suggested quietly.

The next instant he felt his feet raked out from under him, and as he hit the floor, the hard sole of a boot crashed into the side of his head!

Chapter 3

Stunned by the brutal kick, Paul lay with his head at an angle against the bar. The roaring pain in his head failed to dull his reflexes. He caught the booted foot and twisted with all the power of his wide shoulders. Cursing, Stebbins spun and crashed to the floor. Paul rolled away from the bar. Miles was on the other side of him. He kept thinking of that.

He crouched erect unsteadily, eyes blurred. Miles came at him, his fists cocked. Paul was in the open. He backed toward the far wall. He had to keep his tormentors in front of him. Miles closed in. A fist hammered against Paul's ribs, and then his pent-up fury loosed itself. He jabbed and cut Miles' square-cut face. There was a spurt of blood as Miles gave ground. Paul hit him again and watched him fall.

Stebbins was up then, circling. Gasping, Paul felt hopeless and tricked. He was still in the open, with his enemies on either side of him. He moved into Stebbins, felt Stebbins' fists rake and bruise his face. Strangely, the blows served to clear his head. He threw a punch at Stebbins' stomach, and as his guard came

TWISTED TRAILS 53

down, smashed another blow into Stebbins' mouth, drawing blood. Stebbins backed up, spitting blood and yelling at Miles to close in from behind.

The barroom was filling up now. The miners were straggling down the hill, their pockets fat with pay. As the news of the fight was relayed back up the straggling line, the miners broke into a run. This was better than they had bargained for—a grudge fight to start off the celebration. They crowded into the room, shouting and shoving, placing bets upon the outcome.

Addie, still in the dining room, kept her place, her head bowed on her hands. She heard every blow, and she winced with them. There was nothing she could do but let it go on. Paul Scott was a man born for battle, and he had to fight until he was top man or broken.

Paul felt his fury cool. He was conscious of the filling room; he heard shouts as troopers came in to mingle with the miners. He rushed Stebbins, taking punishment and dealing it, until Stebbins was against a table. Paul felt the blood dripping off his chin, tasted it warm and salty in his mouth. Stebbins was bleeding, too. He slid around the table, collided with a chair and fell over it backwards.

Paul turned, puzzled that Miles did not come at him from the rear. Through sweat-glazed eyes he saw that Alonzo Finch held a gun in his hand, daring anyone to make odds, holding Miles back out of the way. Before Paul could grasp just what was happening, he felt a boot heel crash into his back, sending him gasping and staggering to his knees.

He braced himself on his knuckles, sucking to get back his breath. Then Stebbins was riding his back, forcing him down. Stebbins' hands were in his hair, lifting his head to smash his face against the floor.

Before Stebbins could slam his face against the rough planks, Paul's lean body twisted, spun over, and he had his knees across Stebbins' chest and was looking down into Stebbins' bloody face. Methodically he pounded, bruised, battered that face until Stebbins stopped squirming.

Then he rose unsteadily, shaking the sweat from his eyes. He raked his hand across his face, and it came away oily with blood. He focused his eyes carefully until he found Miles. The miners were cheering and stamping, paying off bets and making others on the next round. They recognized in Paul a fighter who finished a job or went down to defeat.

Breathing like a leaky bellows, Paul said, "All right, Alonzo; let him go."

Alonzo said, "Take a breather, Paul; you've earned it."

"Let him go!" Paul repeated.

Finch, a man to give another his head, shoved Miles roughly out on the floor. Miles came out un-

TWISTED TRAILS 55

balanced. He was still trying to find the balls of his feet when Paul hit him the first time. Miles went down close to Stebbins' prostrate form. Two men grabbed Stebbin's feet and pulled him off to one side.

Miles lay for a moment, propped on an elbow, and a switch seemed to turn in his brain. He rose and charged, head low, fists battering.

In the dining room, standing on one of the tables, Norah Young watched the fight, and it sickened her. Because Paul had sided a helpless old man, because he had done the right and decent thing, he was forced to suffer. Aaron was her friend and her father's friend.

Paul waited for Miles' lowered head to come close; then he brought his knee up into the man's face. At the same time he swung his fist, sending Miles down upon his buttocks. Miles swayed there, dazed. With a queer look on his face, he crawled desperately away and stumbled out the back door.

Paul was unable to comprehend that it was over. The miners were jostling and cheering him. As the heat and fury drained away, pain flooded in. He moved unsteadily, held upright by the packed bodies. Then, miraculously, Addie was by his side, taking his arm, leading him through a side door into the kitchen.

There was a small room off the kitchen containing a cot, on which the night cook cat-napped between orders, and on this cot Addie forced Paul to lie. Not until his beaten and bruised body relaxed did he realize how spent he was. Yet he didn't like being fussed over by Addie. A cold dunking would clear his head and stop the bleeding.

"Here, drink this," Addie said, her arm under his head.

The whiskey burned his cut lips like fire but caused a warm glow in his stomach.

"Thanks," he said, lying back.

There was the sound of quick footsteps, and Norah appeared at the foot of the bed. Tears glistened in her eyes.

"Oh, Paul, Paul—" she began.

Addie stepped between them. "You'd better leave, Norah. Don't burden him with dramatics now."

"Burden?" Norah said vaguely. "I want to help him."

"How? By pushing your way in here?"

Enmity hung in the air. Paul could feel it, and he didn't want to cope with it just then. He wanted no grief, no pity.

"Let her alone, Addie," he said. Then to Norah, "You'd better go home, Norah. This is no place for you."

"I've been here before," she pleaded.

"Today is pay day, and the men will play rough. Go on home."

"If that's what you want," Norah said stiffly, and

TWISTED TRAILS 57

he knew she felt thrust out and discarded. She turned, unable to control the sob that shook her. Paul felt something twist in him at the sound.

Addie had warm water and cloths, and she was washing the blood off his face and out of his hair. The warm water dulled the pain which was simmering down into one big hurt. He lay with his eyes closed, trying to piece things together.

Addie, gently salving his cuts, said firmly, "This particular quarrel is ended—at least the fighting part of it."

"Miles ran out, but he wasn't licked," Paul said, feeling his face smart when he talked.

"But I tell you you'll never have to use your fists on those two again. I know."

Paul frowned. "I whipped them yesterday, and they came back."

"They were drunk. They wanted another chance, and now they've had it. They'll accept the decision as far as fists go."

"What do you mean by that, Addie?"

"There are lots of ways to get back at a man without getting hurt. You'll have to watch yourself from now on," Addie warned him.

"How did you ever get dragged into this business, Addie?" Paul asked.

"I wasn't dragged in," she said. "I came in with my eyes open because I wanted to. I was luckier than most."

"How?" he asked, leading her on.

"Aren't you prying?"

"You don't have to tell me anything."

"I know it, but I feel myself wanting to tell you. I'm afraid it would bore you."

"Try me."

"Well, I was raised in Colorado on a homestead on which my folks tried to ranch. The earth there God made for other things, lizards and rocks mostly. We all worked so hard for practically nothing that I vowed as a small girl to find some way, any way, to get free of such a life. My mother killed herself with work, and I couldn't stand it any more.

"I was sixteen then. The next time we drove to town for supplies, I looked up Mike Pugmire, who owned the fanciest saloon in town, and asked him for a job. Mike eyed me familiarly to see if I'd wince, but I gritted my teeth and took it. I showed him my legs; they were all right. So he gave me a job and advised me to learn to dance. I had a rather appealing voice, and the men liked my singing.

"Then I met Carter Grievy. There was a man! He was older than me by quite a bit, but he did things in grand style. You know, I never was sure if we were legally married. We were hitched by a wandering preacher. It worked out all right, though, and Carter taught me how to take care of myself and this

TWISTED TRAILS

business. We lost a horse one day not long after we started the Lone Chance. Carter went down to the Ute village to inquire about it. He never came back, and no trace of him could be found. The only proof we had he was dead were his watch and a fancy belt he always wore. They were later found in a tribe in New Mexico by a man who recognized them."

"You make it sound very simple. And now?"

"Now what?" Addie asked.

"Well, a person's life doesn't end—not while they're alive."

"Look, my friend," Addie said softly, "life is doled out to us in slices and morsels. A day's ration at a time, and no one knows what tomorrow's fare might be."

"I heard the name Severs," Paul said, his eyes closed. "Your man?"

"I don't know," she admitted slowly. "Right now he's not even his own man. Alonzo Finch has some kind of power over him, I don't know what."

"Finch is a weasel—a sucker, stealing others' lives to live by. He did side me in the fight out there, though."

"His type of man would do that," Addie agreed. "In the first place, it built him up in the eyes of the crowd. In the second, he owed you a favor for what you did the other day. Now the score is evened, watch him!"

"I'm here to watch him, and take him back with me. If you ever hear of him leaving, Addie, let me know at once."

The sun was setting now, sending a shaft of light across the room from the high, small window. In that shaft of light the dust in the air roiled and flowed like quicksilver.

"I'd better get back to business," Addie said. "It looks like a big night."

Paul lay for a time, getting used to the soreness of his body. At last he rose, put on his hat and went out through the dining room to the front porch. The sun had gone down, and the dusk was thickening, but a huge fire leaped and roared in front of the building.

The light of the flames, mixing with the gray dusk, cast a strange pinkish glow upon the faces of the men. It seemed to flow from the sky, where the sun had left a banner of color, streaked and furbished with red and orange and yellow. The warmth of the day still lingered, vying with the heat of the fire.

The circling men, some with bottles in their hands, one or two with hands on the shoulders of Addie's girls, watched the moving drama. There was an outcropping of limestone that had been blasted and shaped into a platform with a solid rock wall at the back. Upon this platform labored the drilling teams. Holes from other contests pierced the rock. The crowd cheered and strained to help their favorites.

Paul watched the drilling teams swinging their hammers in relentless, ringing blows. Stripped to the waist, their sweaty bodies appeared oily in the firelight; their biceps bulged and stretched, and the muscles of their backs writhed like snakes. One man crouched beside the holes, turning the long drill that bit its way into the rock, while the man with the double jack swung the heavy hammer faster and faster!

There was a steady ring of steel upon steel; pause to pour water into the hole to muddy the drillings; a swift change of steel as the mud was scooped from the hole with a scraper. There was an earnestness and precision about the two teams of drillers that was amazing.

Paul was conscious of another person close to him in the darkening shadows of the porch.

"Quite a big commotion here tonight," Morgan's gruff voice said.

Paul tensed. From Morgan he expected nothing but enmity.

"Yeah, big," he said, thinking of his own contribution to the fun.

"I won a nice little bet on you this afternoon," Morgan went on affably, his tone even. "I'm a betting man, but I like a square deal. I still think your friend Finch is a cheat, but I'm glad I didn't kill him.

Thanks for butting in."

"He's not my friend. I figured you might hate my guts for what I did," Paul said.

"I never hold a grudge unless the cause keeps galling me: I could use a man like you."

"I'm already bought," Paul said shortly. "Besides, I could never do that work." He indicated the drillers still moving like well-oiled machines in the flickering firelight. It was getting quite dark by now, and most of the light came from the flames. "It beats me how they can see what they're doing."

Morgan grunted. "Look at 'em, working like mad to drill a hole into nowhere. They never break their backs when they're really working underground. I ought to know; I'm the daylight shift boss. That firelight is more than enough for them to drill by. They're used to a couple of candles stuck in the wall when they drill in the mine."

"What they're doing looks like quite an achievement to me," Paul confessed.

"There are some good men there," Morgan said. "Fewker and Migallo, the team on the left, have won matches in most of the camps of the territory. Calder and Tanner are riding them hard, though. If they don't get tricked out of it, they might win this match."

"Tricked out of it?" Paul asked. "How?"

"Watch the men crowding in close around the rock.

TWISTED TRAILS 63

They'll try to slip in a dull steel on them if they can. Calder's backers are watching them, though. I've got a hundred riding on Calder and Tanner," Morgan said. "Had to give three to five odds."

The longest of the set of drills was nearly buried in the rock now, and the men began to shout in a frenzy of encouragement to their favorites. Even from the porch it could be seen that the match was close. Then, across the yard, Paul saw Norah standing in the front rank of the men. Beside her, his hand possessively on her arm, stood Alonzo Finch.

He started off the porch, but Morgan kept him from going.

"Wait a minute, Scott," Morgan said. "The fun is just beginning. You see the miners have to put on a big enough show so the railroad hands can't top it. You should see them perform on pay day."

"Certainly they don't drill holes?" Paul asked, keeping his eyes on Norah and Finch.

"No, but they have their own battle. They drive rail spikes. I've seen them start twenty of them the length of a tie, and drive the lot of them with twenty strokes. That's what I call swinging a maul."

There was a fresh outburst from the crowd now as the drilling match ended. Paul saw the double-jackers standing on their spread legs, the big hammers slack in their tired hands. He heard a new shout from the men as the holes were measured.

"Attention! Attention!" a man shouted. He stood on the rock between the two drilling teams. "The winners are Fewker and Migallo!"

Paul grinned at Morgan, "You lost some skin there," he said.

Morgan shrugged. "I'll get it back before the night's over," he promised without changing expression.

Then Paul saw a new commotion in the crowd nearer the porch. He caught sight of "Big-head" Larson, his shambling, stooped body being pushed and badgered by a bunch of men who were yelling at him, offering to give him a cut of bets if he did something or other. Larson appeared disinterested. Then Paul saw that one of the men in the crowd carried a rifle, and his interest increased.

"What's going on there?"

"Big-head gets his moment of glory. Watch him. He always makes them argue with him; he has to be begged. In the end he'll do just what they want him to."

As though at a signal, the crowd melted away at the end of the yard, leaving a clear path to the small hill not far off. Somebody rolled a stump to the drilling platform. Paul saw the men near the porch force a rifle into Big-head's paw-like hands.

The rifle looked dangerous in the possession of Big-head. But once he had the gun, Big-head appeared to grow straighter; his head came up and he looked about with a curious grin on his thick lips. He had the dedicated, inspired look of a child with a long-coveted toy. But this was no toy; it was a rifle of the latest type, a Winchester repeater!

The gun alone was enough to create interest, but something Big-head was going to do with the gun appeared to be the important thing. Paul had never fired a repeater himself.

"The six—put up the six!" somebody yelled.

At the same time somebody added dry fuel to the fire, causing it to leap and surge, washing the gathering in a bright yellow light. Paul could see the men fifty yards away fastening a six of hearts to the butt end of the stump. Paul realized it was a target.

Paul was still not sure whether this whole affair was a joke or not. Even in daylight, the small playing card would have made a difficult target. In the uncertain light of the fire, it would be almost impossible to hit. As though in answer to his thought, two men stepped forward and placed a burning candle in the rock on either side of the card, close enough to illuminate it.

"It's a ritual," Morgan said suddenly.

Paul was startled by the interruption, because he, like the others, was watching Big-head, fascinated by the man's changed appearance. Big-head waved the men back and braced the rifle against his bullish shoulder. His slitted eye glittered on the sight, and the rifle jumped into roaring, flaming life.

The men near the target chanted as the shots flared forth, "One, Two! Three! Four! Five! Six!" The rest of the crowd had taken up the chant and, as the echo of the last shot died, a tense silence fell upon the men. Then the card was removed and passed with expressions of awe from hand to hand. When Paul finally saw it, he was impressed. The six bullets had struck the card, not completely obliterating the six hearts, but following their pattern.

The crowd began to break up now, paying off bets and moving into the bar to quench their thirsts. Paul suddenly remembered Norah, but she was not there. Neither was Alonzo Finch. He heard Morgan mumble something at his side and drift away, but he did not follow. He hurried across the yard, squirming his way through the flowing crowd, still unable to see Norah. He went to the rack where the horses were tied. When he saw Norah's pinto there his misgivings increased. Somebody had kicked the fire into new life, and as the light reached out, Paul caught a glimpse of figures in the shadows at the side of the building.

He moved over so the corner of the building would shield him and then quietly approached the spot. As he turned the corner, he was close enough to see them clearly. Norah was standing with her

TWISTED TRAILS 67

back against the wall, and Finch stood in front of her, an arm against the wall on either side of her. Paul couldn't tell what they were saying, but when he heard Norah's nervous laugh, he realized that Finch was impressing her.

Paul stepped toward them, caught Finch's shoulder and forced him around.

"All right, Alonzo," Paul said. "It's time I took Norah home."

Alonzo Finch glared at him, his face sharp with anger, but the next moment he had regained his composure.

"Paul," he said, "you're getting to be a nuisance. I don't intend to put up with you forever. You came to take me back to Oklahoma. Well, fill your brag, or quit bothering me. Frankly, you look terrible with your face puffed and cut like it is. I'm sure Norah would find me better company. I"ll take her home."

"Alonzo, I've had enough fighting for one day," Paul said gravely, "but if I have to, I'll fight again. This is no place for Norah, and you're not fit company for her."

Finch backed off a step, his head cocked a little to the side. Norah pushed herself away from the building. The sight of Paul's cut and battered face hurt her deeply. Realizing that he must not incur more punishment, she stepped between them.

"I'm going home with Paul, Alonzo," she said

quietly, but with a hint of apology in her voice. "Good night."

"Good night, Norah," Finch said politely. "Uriah should teach his 'hands' to keep in their place."

Paul grimly refused to honor the remark with a reply. He took Norah's arm and led her quietly toward the line of horses.

Chapter 4

Addie Grievy, stepping from the wooden tub, rubbed herself vigorously with the towel. She inspected her flawless skin in the long mirror and felt her old discontent rise. Why had she picked up with Lieth Severs? Perhaps it was his need for her that held her to him. Why couldn't she have waited for a man like Paul?

She dressed nervously. She was older than Paul, but that made no difference. She brushed her hair, piled it on top of her head. Now that she had made up her mind, there was no time to lose. Even tonight might be too late. She must warn Paul of danger, and see that he acted on her advice.

What sort of danger? She wasn't sure herself. Paul was not wanted in the valley by certain elements, and he still had the enmity of the two troopers he had whipped. Major Hornaby had made some very pointed remarks the last time he had visited her.

She dressed in her riding habit. Paul had not come

back to the Lone Chance since the night of the fight, so she would have to swallow her pride and go to him. Giving herself a last satisfied inspection, she went downstairs, where she asked Big-head Larson to saddle her horse and bring him around front. Since Grievy had died, she had not done much riding. The business had required too much of her time, and then, too, Lieth did not care to ride.

She approached the Young ranch with some trepidation, because she had never met Helen Young. She had seen her, to be sure, but there had never been any word spoken between them. If Norah was there, it would be easier. It amused her somewhat to discover that she was nervous.

She dismounted and walked to the porch, looking eagerly around, hoping to see Paul. Her hand trembled as she raised it; then her delicate knuckles rapped sharply on the panel. At first there was no response, and she had the uncomfortable feeling that she was being watched.

She knocked once more. Soon footsteps sounded inside the house and came to a halt just behind the door. Still the door remained closed, and she was going to knock again when the door opened and Helen Young stood there, her head up, her shoulders back, and a strange, opaque shield over his eyes.

"Yes?" she inquired in a tone normally reserved for a tramp, a cowpoke, or an Indian begger.

TWISTED TRAILS 71

"I'm Mrs. Grievy—Addie Grievy," Addie began.

"I'm quite aware who you are."

"I had hoped we might be friends," Addie said lamely.

"Don't you think that is presumptuous on your part?" Helen asked. "It is unfortunate my own daughter sees fit to spend time in your place. When her eyes are opened—"

Addie felt her anger rising.

"Are you so confident about your judgment of people? I know that Alonzo Finch has been coming down here this week," Addie said, keeping her voice low. She saw a strange, defensive look come into Helen's eyes at the mention of Finch.

"Mr. Finch is a gentleman," Helen said, and added pointedly, "He comes to see Norah."

"So I assumed. Alonzo is no fool. Gentleman he may be on the surface, but if you knew men like I know them, you'd realize there's a skunk odor about him."

"Why—why, you insulting person!"

"What makes you feel so pure and superior, Mrs. Young?" Addie asked with more pity than anger. "This is the West—not Kansas City or St. Louis. If I had a daughter like Norah, Finch is the last man I'd want her interested in."

"I think I can handle my own affairs," Helen said. "I suppose you'd rather I'd encourage that new man,

Paul Scott, or are you after him yourself?"

"I think Norah would be a very lucky girl to get a man like Paul Scott. But don't fret. He won't be here very long. I came here to give him a warning."

"Against me, I suppose," Helen snapped.

"Don't be so touchy," Addie said

"I don't relish being insulted at my own door. I keep no rein on Paul Scott, and I don't know where he is."

"May I talk with Norah, then?"

"Norah has gone riding with Mr. Finch. I'd rather you didn't come here any more. I have my pride."

Addie closed her eyes and clenched her fists. This stuffy, proud woman dared insult her, and she could not strike back. How could one pierce such a garment of self-righteousness? Addie turned away, ashamed and angered, and then a voice startled her.

"What's the matter, Addie?" Paul asked, swinging around the corner of the house.

Helen slammed the door and disappeared.

"She—insulted me. I—"

Paul, hearing the hurt in Addie's voice, put a kindly arm about her shoulder, and led her into the deep shadows of the orchard.

"It's all right, Addie. Helen Young is harming only herself."

"She'll get in trouble mixing up with Finch," Addie said.

"I've tried to tell Norah, but her mother is urging her to see Finch. If he harms that girl, I'll kill him," he threatened.

"Then how will you clear yourself back home?" she reminded him. "You need Finch alive."

Paul scratched his head. "I reckon I didn't think about that. I'll just have to watch him, I guess. If Norah is in love with him—"

"Don't be a fool, Paul. Norah is falling in love, but not with Alonzo Finch."

Paul was silent.

"Wake up, Paul. She's falling in love with you."

"You're wrong, Addie," he said. "She avoids me."

"Of course; she's a woman. You can't expect her to throw herself at you."

"You mean if a woman loves a man, she avoids him?"

"She hopes he'll run after her."

Paul shook his head. "Sound mixed up to me."

"Take my word for it. I know. I'm a woman."

Mentally Paul agreed with that. Addie was a woman clear through, a handsome, uncomplicated woman. It was her forthrightness that attracted him.

"Okay. Even if Norah wanted me to court her, I wouldn't have the right," he said.

"You mean there's a girl—another girl?"

"No, I'm free that way, but there's a cloud on my past, a cloud that only Finch can clear up. I may not get him to do it, but I'm going to try. When the warrant comes, if the marshal will deputize me, I aim to take Finch back in handcuffs if necessary. Why should Norah be dragged through all that trouble?"

"If she loves you, it won't be trouble to her," Addie said, her eyes on the ground.

"Why should you tell me all this, Addie?"

"I'm not sure, Paul. Maybe I'm just punishing myself. I know how Norah feels, because I like you a lot myself," Addie said lamely. "If I thought there was any chance—"

"Addie, all I can tell you is what I said before. Right now I'm not a man for any woman to get mixed up with. You didn't come here to tell me all this. Why did you come?"

"I really came to warn you, Paul."

"Warn me?"

"There's a plot on foot to get you out of the way, either dead or alive. I've heard talk around the Lone Chance. I've pieced things together."

"And what did you get?"

"There's a lot of liquor being bought that isn't drunk in the Lone Chance, Paul. There are other shipments coming into the railroad camp. There's been liquor turning up in the Indian village, and that's illegal. Liquor and Indians don't mix."

"That's a job for the army." Paul shrugged. "I

can't do anything about it."

"I know it's a job for the army, and Hornaby will try to stop it. It won't be easy. I've heard that he can't even keep liquor off the post. Just this morning a sentry was asleep on duty. He was drunk. Hornaby threatened to make an example of him."

"Of course he's got to discipline the man, but he can't be too tough on him."

"He might let the man off easier if the smuggler were caught. He could make an example of the smuggler instead," Addie said.

"There isn't a war on."

"Hornaby's given orders that anybody seen trying to enter the camp without permission is to be shot on sight."

Paul whistled softy. Honraby had impressed him as being vain, but he did not think he was a fool.

"Why are you telling me all this, Addie?"

"Because I'm afraid they've picked you as the smuggler."

"Me? That's crazy."

"Maybe it is, and maybe it isn't," Addie said. "I came to tell you not to be seen around the camp after dark."

"Look, Addie, don't fret yourself. I'm not likely to go to the post after dark. I know no one there but Sergeant McCune."

"Even if you're called for any reason, refuse to

go," Addie warned him. "Those troopers, Miles and Stebbins, are still unhappy."

"They'll not lure me to the post."

Addie looked up, and their eyes met. Even in the dusk, her eyes were bright and probing. Paul returned her look, and because of her intensity, he put an arm about her and drew her close, feeling her tremble. Before he released her, she reached up, drew down his head and kissed him on the mouth. Then she hurried away like a woman who had let a man look into her heart.

Paul heard Addie ride away. She had left him with a feeling of sadness, for she had revealed herself as woman unfulfilled and searching. Paul shook his head slowly, knowing he could not help her.

Absorbed in his thoughts, he failed to hear the light footsteps until Norah stood before him. He looked at her in surprise, as though she had materialized out of thin air. He restrained an impulse to put his arms about her. The way she stood there some distance from him, he knew that something was wrong.

Because the silence was awkward, he hazarded, "Where have you been, Norah?"

"Riding," she said shortly.

There was a challenge in the angle of her chin, and he wanted to reach out and straighten her head.

"Alone?" he asked her, as stingy with words as she was.

"No. I was with Alonzo."

"After all I told you about him?"

"Let's just say he's done nothing to prove your charges."

"I hope he never does, Norah."

"Why should you be concerned? You have Addie—Alonzo has warned her against you. He warned me, too. He told me some dreadful things. He dares you to deny them."

"Do you believe what he told you?"

"I don't know. What was Addie doing here? I saw you kiss her," Norah said, trying hard to control her voice. "I was in back of those bushes outside the gate."

"Do you know why Addie came?"

"I could guess. I saw her in your arms."

"You could be wrong, you know," Paul said. "Addie came to warn me."

"Warn you?"

"It appears I'm to be the victim of a trap," Paul explained.

For a moment there was silence, and he knew the girl was struggling with a problem.

"I think Addie made that up, Paul, to have an excuse to come and see you. It worked very well, didn't it?"

"Suppose she's telling the truth? Do you think I should ignore her warning?"

A new, deeper note came into Norah's voice. "No, Paul, of course not. If anything more happened to you—"

"Yes?"

"I'd feel awful."

"I'm glad to hear that, Norah. But you'd still have Finch."

"Yes," she said slowly, lowering her eyes, "yes, I'd still have Alonzo, wouldn't I?" Her tone was mocking.

Paul felt worry dog him. "What did Alonzo tell you about me, Norah?"

She kept her eyes lowered. "I know they were lies, the things he said."

"Like what?" Paul insisted.

"Well, he said you came from a family of crooks. He said one of your brothers was lynched for murder and the other one was run out of town. He said you stole a lot of money and ruined a man's life and that's why you're running away." She spoke the charges so swiftly the words ran together.

She was only a blur in the light now, and could not see his face. For this, Paul was glad. He knew his face was white, his eyes sharp and hateful. He mulled over ways of defending himself, of watering down the charges, so that they did not seem so blunt. Unconsciously he took a step toward her.

Before the step was completed, a rifle shot ripped

TWISTED TRAILS 79

open the night! Paul felt his hat jerked from his head. The whine of a bullet screamed and stopped as the bullet clawed its way into the trunk of a tree. Paul fell forward, dragging the girl down with him.

There was a faint sound of bushes rattling. Still Paul didn't move. He and the girl would be fair targets if they were on their feet. Then a sound came from some distance, a sound of feet running.

Paul leaped up without a word and vaulted the fence. He lost his footing as his high heels hit the earth, and he cursed. For another instant he stood, crouched, then heard a crashing in the brush to his right. He plunged that way, no longer trying to keep hidden. Whoever had shot at him was now panicked by failure and thought only of escape. Paul lunged on into the thickets of rabbit brush and greasewood, trying to get a glimpse of his assailant, but the brush was too tall.

He ran into a rough section of rocks and felt his leg double under him. He cursed aloud. He had twisted his ankle, but he could still navigate. He went on unsteadily and came into an open space, where a movement ahead of him caught his eye, a high dark shadow. He tried to find the outline of a man in in it, but he could not. Then it dawned on him. It was a horse!

He followed the animal, thinking there might be a man nearby. The horse evidently belonged to his assailant, who was undoubtedly afraid to mount for fear of being seen above the brush.

The trail led in the general direction of the Lone Chance. Whoever had plotted to kill him must have come from there. Paul decided to head for the Lone Chance when he suddenly discovered he had lost his gun. Furious at himself for his carelessness, he tried to think where it could be. The most logical place to search would be the rocky place where he had turned his ankle. For a moment he thought of going on without a gun, but an inner voice of caution warned him to go back and get it. Panting, he hurried back along the trail, hopeful he could find the spot where he had fallen. Luckily, his sense of direction served him well, and he soon reached the rocks. Even then it took some time to locate his revolver.

Armed once more, he turned and headed toward the Lone Chance. If his pursuer had taken refuge there, he would already have arrived. There was little need to wind himself. He changed course and made an attempt to capture the roaming horse. To his surprise, the animal stood stone still, listening to Paul's low, soothing words.

Paul mounted. He knew this cayuse; it was one he had seen Finch ride. However, that proved little. It was one of Addie's horses which she rented out. In fact he had seen Addie herself riding the animal. Because conjecture was fruitless, he cleared his

TWISTED TRAILS

mind and rode toward the Lone Chance at a brisk trot.

Still cautious, he dismounted some distance from the Lone Chance and approached the back of the building on foot. His attacker, his panic having subsided now that he had cover, might still try to complete his job. Paul stopped by the stable in back of the saloon and studied the big building. He circled until he was near the wall and crept toward the front porch. He vaulted up and headed for the door.

Cautiously, he approached the bright rectangle of light that fell from the open doorway. Feeling of his gun, he stepped inside, where his eyes picked out three or four miners bellying up to the bar and discarded them. The miners had no quarrel with him, and men who labored hard for a living did not accept Judas money. He did not see Addie, and he was glad, because this was his job and he wanted no interference. Across the room, Alonzo Finch had his attention fixed upon a card game, and Paul decided it was a good place to start.

Finch didn't see him until Paul reached the table. Finch looked up with unconcealed surprise that congealed into naked malice. If eyes could kill, Paul would have been a dead man. He realized then how difficult would be the job of ever taking Finch back to Oklahoma. Even as he thought that, Paul was studying the men about the table, none of whom showed any signs of having been on a recent chase.

Paul asked bluntly, "Did anyone see a man dodge in here just now?"

Finch resumed the cynical, mocking manner he wore so well.

"You are about the busiest man I ever did see, Paul," Alonzo said evenly. "Where's your hat? How come you're puffing like a leaky tea kettle?"

Conscious of the amused glances of the other card players, Paul said grimly, "Somebody tried to kill me tonight. I trailed him this way."

"Now who would want to do a thing like that?" Finch jeered.

"Maybe you can say?" Paul countered.

"Paul, you're developing a persecution complex. I suppose somebody witnessed the try?"

"That's right. Norah. She was lucky she didn't stop the slug."

Paul saw the tightening in Finch's face, and knew he had struck close to home.

"I warned her against you," Finch said honestly. "If she gets hurt because of you—"

"That's something I'd like to settle with you later," Paul said. "She'll not get hurt unless somebody else hurts her. And I'll kill the man who does. Now I want to know, did a man come in here just before me?"

"Ask the others," Finch suggested, turning his

attention to his cards.

Paul looked inquiringly around the table, but the only answer was shaking heads. Then he remembered the balcony above the front porch. An active man could easily shinny up to the balcony and enter the second floor through one of the windows. Aware of Finch's furtive look, Paul turned toward the stairs and started up into the dimness above.

Chapter 5

Paul reached the upstairs hall and stood quietly in the shadows until his eyes adjusted themselves to the faint light filtered up from below. Slowly he pushed himself away from the wall, his eyes busy in the gloom. He made out the rectangular outlines of three doors on either side of the corridor. Soundlessly he approached the first door and paused. He heard a man's low voice, and a girl's answering laugh. He turned away.

The next room across the hall was dark, with the door slightly ajar. Quietly he entered, cursing the squeak of a hinge. His hand explored the bed and found it empty. There was a hazy thread of light under the next door, and he raised his knuckles hesitantly and knocked. There was the swish of clothing inside, and when the door opened, a girl, dressed in a bright silk kimono, was silhouetted against the light.

"I'm looking for a man," Paul said.

TWISTED TRAILS 85

"So am I," she countered challengingly.

"Did you hear anybody come up here in the past fifteen minutes?" Paul questioned insistently.

"I don't pay no attention to who comes or goes."

"Maybe on the balcony, you could have heard him. Your room faces on the balcony, doesn't it?"

"So what?"

"I'm just asking a question. A man tried to kill me. I want to know why."

"I don't know anything about anybody, and if I did, why should I tell you?"

Paul backed away, angered and puzzled by the girl's animosity. He moved on to the last door down the hall, put his ear to the panel and made out heavy breathing.

Unfolding his stock knife, Paul forced the long blade under the door stop and pried it away from the jamb. Then he pushed the blade in through the crack of the door and slid the bolt of the lock back. Standing to one side, he swung the door open. The window leading out on the balcony was still raised, and enough light entered the room to reveal the outlines of a big man under the cover.

Paul, easing his gun around, approached the bed. He stood over the prone figure. Slipping his hand under the cover, he felt the man's clothing, still damp with sweat. He felt a bulge in the pocket of the shirt. It was a purse, which he took out and slipped into his own pocket. This was his man. Still the prostrate form made no protest. Paul moved to the commode and, striking a match, lit the candle that stood there. Then he turned to the bed and looked down on Big-head Larson's shaggy head.

Twining his hand in Larson's hair, Paul lifted the big head and slammed it back on the pillow. Even as he did so, his mind swiftly went back to that night a week ago when Big-head had shot the spots off the six of hearts.

"What yuh want?" Big-head growled in his barrel chest. Can't a man get no sleep around here?"

"Get up, Larson!" Paul said harshly.

"Go 'way. I ain't got nuthin' for you."

Paul struck the man's bristly face. "Who sent you out to kill me?" Paul demanded.

Larson was making sounds like an angry bear. He half rose from the pillow in defense.

"I don't know what you're talkin' about."

Paul struck him again, harder. He had to get the answer now, before Larson could report to the man who had hired him.

"Come on; talk. I'll knock your teeth down your throat."

"Let me go!" Larson snarled.

Paul, not wanting to attract the men from downstairs, drew his knife and held the point at Larson's short, thick throat.

"Come on; tell me who sent you. Was it Finch? Was it Stebbins or Miles? Talk!"

"Let me go!"

"I'll fix it so you'll never talk again," Paul threatened, putting pressure on the knife.

Big-head moved with the agility of a cat. He drew up his leg and stiff-legged his boot into Paul's stomach. The attack was so unexpected it sent Paul gasping and groaning across the floor. He fell, striking his head against the sharp, hard corner of the commode. The candle was snuffed out, but it was a deeper darkness that swallowed Paul. . . .

When he came to, he lay a moment stunned. Vaguely, he remembered what had happened. He had come in so big, so brave, and he had made a fool of himself. His head buzzing with pain, he rose and approached the bed. It was empty. As his head cleared, he listened to the sounds downstairs and out in the corridor. It was apparent that his scuffle with Big-head had not attracted attention. Or had it been purposely ignored? He rubbed his head gingerly and, climbing through the window, leaned against the wall of the house on the balcony.

His eyes fingered the darkness below and found no one. He saw the dim shapes of brush and juniper etched against the blackness of the distance, but nothing moved. As he stood there, his head cleared and his body relaxed. He went quietly to the railing of the balcony and crawled over. Wrapping a leg about a post, he slid noiselessly down to the ground. He did not want to face the men in the saloon just then. It would only mean more futile argument. Big-head had shot at him, of that he was sure, but he had yet to prove who was the man behind Big-head.

Warily he walked to the barn in back of the Lone Chance. The saddled horse was gone. Big-head had ridden off.

Paul shook his head and rubbed a hand across his eyes. The pain was subsiding. He had to get home. Norah would be worried. He decided against taking one of Addie's horses without inquiring, and he did not want to meet Addie just then. He wanted to get home, to tell Norah that everything was all right. He started out down the night-dark trail on foot.

He heard horses some distance away. Having escaped once with his life, he did not intend to take another chance. Turning into the brush, he concealed himself and waited. He had not long to wait, his eyes sharp and searching, until he saw a lone rider leading another horse.

"Hello, the trail!" he called.

The rider pulled up so sharply the following horse had to dodge the leader's tail.

"Paul—Paul, are you all right?" Norah asked.

Paul laughed softly. "What happened to you?"

"You're dresesd up fit to scare a Ute brave." Paul

chuckled.

"Oh, I guess I do look funny. Uriah made me take his coat, so I wouldn't be cold. I brought you a horse."

"Thanks, Norah," he said, mounting the spare horse and accepting his hat.

For a moment they rode in silence back toward the ranch, and the stars were a million eyes watching them softly. Paul sucked in the sweet, clean air and felt the weariness of his bones.

"What happened, Paul?" Norah inquired when he remained silent.

"Oh, I chased him through the brush and lost him. He was heading for Addie's. I found him there in an upstairs room. It was Big-head Larson; I'm sure it was him. I tried to scare him into admitting it and telling me who paid him to do it, but he was too fast for me. Slammed a foot into my stomach and knocked me down. I went out like a light. When I came to, he was gone."

A note of fear came into Norah's voice. "Then— you're still in danger?"

"Reckon I am."

"Do you think Alonzo paid that man?"

"I wouldn't know."

"How bad was the crime you say he committed?"

"It wasn't the crime; it was trying to put the blame on me that sent me after him. Money can be repaid, it can be earned, but a man's reputation is something else. Remember the things Finch told you about me?"

"I think they were lies, Paul. Forget them."

Paul felt hard and cold inside. He had been a fool to think he could have this girl, could win her love and respect. There could be no evasions now. He had to stand up and once again face shame and misery for crimes of which he was innocent. Desperately he searched for some means of defense, some way to soften the blow.

"Norah," he asked slowly, knowing she had expected a swift, heated denial, "do you believe that a man's blood is the whole man?"

"What do you mean?" she asked, puzzled.

Paul was sensitive to the surprise in her tone. He could not give her the heated denial she had expected, but he had to make her understand.

"Well," he temporized, "do you believe that the sins of the brothers are visited—"

"If you're quoting scripture, Paul, that reads, 'The sins of the father.'"

"It's the same thing," he said. "In other words, do you believe a curse is inherited by all members of a family?"

She was trying to comprehend; even in the darkness he could tell that. Only the soft pad of the horses' hooves on the dusty trail broke the stillness.

"You mean do I think that one rotten apple

TWISTED TRAILS 91

spoils the barrel?" she asked finally.

"Yes, something like that."

"Well, not if the rotten apple is thrown out. But you're building up defenses against things I haven't accused you of," she added quickly.

Paul wet his lips, which were very dry. His throat was dry, too. Even his mind was dry, brittle dry. How could he explain things so this innocent, protected girl would understand?"

"I'm going to tell you some things you won't like to hear, Norah. I want you to reserve judgment. In a way, Alonzo Finch was right, except that he failed to name himself as the villain of the piece. Finch, from the best family in town, bullied my brothers into stealing, even though he was younger than they were. None of them had to steal. Some perverse devil in their brain wouldn't let them be. They started stealing candy, and ended up stealing money from the bank. Once they rustled cattle from a big trail herd going up to Kansas, and they would have been lynched if my mother had not interceded and offered twice as many cattle as had been stolen. When Seigleman in the bank was killed, Finch helped stir up the mob that lynched by brother, Pete. Larry got out of town. But Finch wasn't through with us. He framed me for the robbery of a shipment of money by luring me to the place where the crime had been committed and planting some of the money at my home. They couldn't get enough evidence to convict me, but I was convicted in the eyes of our friends and neighbors. That's why I've hunted Alonzo Finch to this place; that's why I've got to take him back and make him confess."

"Alonzo said you would tell me all this, just as you have," she said in a small voice.

"He was banking on my honesty. He knew I wouldn't lie to you. I tell you, Norah, I myself am innocent of crime."

If only he had not fallen in love with her, he could have avoided the necessity of telling her anything.

"Do you believe me, Norah?" he pleaded, thankful for the darkness that hid the anguish in his eyes.

"I want to believe you're good, Paul," she said in the same small voice.

The doubt was there. Why shouldn't it be? Truth was something that had to be proven by facts, or accepted by a great love.

"Look, Norah," he said, "nobody's perfect, but I am not a criminal."

They were riding into the ranch yard, and still Norah did not speak. Hoping not to arouse Helen and Uriah, they went around to the kitchen door. There was a lamp burning in the kitchen, and it cast a faint yellow glow through the door glass. Paul looked down into her face, and saw the struggle

TWISTED TRAILS

there. Suddenly she threw her arms about him and sobbed against his chest.

"I love you, Paul," she breathed.

"But you can't quite believe me," he said bitterly. "I'm not asking you to. I'm not accepting your love until I can clear the slate, until I can prove that I have done no wrong."

In spite of his resolution, he held her, but he did not take her lips. Finally she lifted her face and stood away from him.

"You must be hungry," she said. "Come into the kitchen, and I'll get you some food."

Major Hornaby sat in the small office at one end of his quarters and re-read the note that had been slipped under the door. It would be difficult to say who had written the note without going to considerable trouble. This he did not propose to do. It was sufficient that he had the note.

There was a commotion outside, and he looked through the small window to see the morning patrol marching down the company street. Two men were carrying a stretcher on which lay the body of a man. McCune entered the office. His serious expression disturbed Hornaby.

Saluting, McCune said, "Sergeant McCune reporting, sir. The body of a man was found in the brush not five miles from the post."

Major Hornaby's back stiffened. "Who found him?"

"The morning patrol under Lieutenant Skaggs, sir."

"And how was he killed?"

"Arrow. Nice quiet job," McCune answered. "Straight into his heart from the back. I examined him."

"Since when are you doing the doctor's work for him, Mr. McCune? Take the body to the infirmary, have the doctor examine it, and then have him report to me."

"Yes, sir," McCune said.

Before long Dr. Cranny came in, his bloated face twitching. From the multiple folds that swaddled them, his eyes shone like fugitive mice.

"Well, Captain, what did you find?" Major Hornaby asked.

"The deceased had a hole in his back; his heart was pierced," the doctor reported.

It was a report the rawest recruit could have given. Cranny was either getting drunk again, or just sobering up from the last time. There was liquor in the medical stores. He exuded it.

"How long has he been dead?"

Cranny straightened his shoulders, and his face stopped twitching. For a moment professional pride, the almost forgotten will to be a man, shone in his eyes.

"I would say seven to eight hours, Major," the doctor said.

"Have you the arrow that killed him?"

"I have *an* arrow."

"What do you mean by that?"

"I mean I have the arrow that was in the wound. It didn't kill him."

"So what did kill him?"

"He was killed with a knife. The arrow was thrust into the wound to make it look like an Indian had done it."

Hornaby whistled softly and drummed on his desk.

"Is there anything else you can tell me?"

"He showed signs of having been struck in the face, and there was a small cut on his throat."

"Have you examined the Indians in the guardhouse?" Hornaby inquired.

Cranny's face began to contort again. It was as though it were infested with invisible fleas.

"Why should I examine the filthy beggars? I can give you a report on them right now. Lice, dirt, bad diet. The biggest curse they carry is the white man. They're pushed and starved and robbed," Cranny said bitterly.

"All right, all right, Doctor. That'll be all. Tell McCune I want to see him."

For another brief interval, Cranny drummed up a

few shreds of dignity.

"I'm not your striker, Major," he said.

Hornaby sighed. "Oh, go on; get out." He pounded his desk for his striker and sent him after McCune.

McCune entered, and because there was no one else about, he didn't pretend to salute. He pushed his hat to the back of his balding head and spat accurately into the polished brass cuspidor.

"Well, Major," McCune said, "you've got a murder to solve. Happy?"

"Do you think I should ignore it?"

"No. But it's going to be hard to find the hombre who did it."

"We'll decide on that after we've made a try, Sergeant. Was there any kind of positive evidence near where the body was found?"

"I wasn't there," McCune said. "Lieutenant Skaggs was in charge of the patrol. I just picked them up when they reached the post."

"Then why didn't Skaggs report the murder?"

"That, Major, you will have to ask Skaggs."

"Did you talk with him?"

"Yes, I did."

"Come on; don't make me drag it out of you. What did he say?"

"He said they found the man lying as though he had fallen from a horse. There were only the tracks of one horse. Skaggs followed the tracks some distance, and they merged with the tracks of two other horses. Farther on, the tracks of the horses diverged, two of them going toward the Lone Chance, the other toward the village."

"What do you make out of that story?"

"Why, I haven't tried to make anything out of it. It's your baby."

"Look, Mac, why don't you grow up? Your resentment of my authority is a bit childish. After all, it wasn't my fault you didn't get that commission."

"Major, I know you failed to recommend me, and I know why. You wouldn't get to first base without me. I've been pulling chestnuts for you for years."

"I don't care to discuss that now, Mac," Hornaby said evasively. "I want you to go out and release the Utes who were brought in drunk last night. I think they're sober enough to go home now."

"Release them? Why, they may be the murderers!" McCune said.

"The doctor said the man has been dead for eight hours. That means he was killed about midnight. The Utes were brought in not later than ten last night. They were already crazy drunk, whooping and hollering."

"You can't take Doc's word for it," McCune countered. "Suppose these Indians went out to meet the man, and he had hooch? Suppose they put an arrow in his back, then took the whiskey?"

"That's too many supposes for a night as dark as last night, Sergeant," Hornaby said. "Suppose you do as you're ordered and leave this to me. You told me it was my baby," Hornaby said.

"Some babies are born with teeth, Major. Be careful this one doesn't bite you."

"Release the Indians."

"So you're not going to question them?"

"What could they know about it? They were drunk."

"They might know a lot about it. You want to solve the case, don't you? Don't tell me that by some magic insight you've already discovered the murderer?"

"McCune," Hornaby snapped, "get out of here. When I want any more of your opinions, I'll ask for them."

McCune's impertinence always left Major Hornaby with a feeling of guilt and discontent.

His striker came in with a peculiar look on his face, a look that Hornaby resented. The young trooper made him feel guilty of some foul deed.

"What is it, Mr. Wagner?" Hornaby asked impatiently.

"There's a girl outside who wants to see you?"

"A girl?"

"Yes, sir. One of Addie's girls. Gladys."

"What does she want?"

"She won't say, sir," Wagner said. "She wants to

see you personally."

"All right, Wagner. Get that look off your face. I didn't send for her. Let her come in."

Unconsciously, Hornaby straightened his tunic and ran his slim hand over his hair. When he went to Addie's, he went to see Addie. She was a woman a man could talk to without having to revert to banal vulgarities. He remembered Gladys, a nice-looking girl, but one with a chip on her shoulder. Then the door opened and Gladys came in. In her hand she carried very carefully some object wrapped loosely in a cloth.

Chapter 6

As Paul rode the load of leafy, sweet-smelling alfalfa toward the post, his mind was everywhere but on the road. He tried to straighten out the events of the night before and fit them into some kind of chronological order. When he had left Norah, glum and silent in the kitchen, he had found Eglund already asleep in the bunkhouse. This morning when he had gone into the kitchen for breakfast, Eglund had already eaten and left.

It was doubtful that Eglund had been the prowler at the ranch, but Eglund might know who the prowler was. There was even a chance that Sodek might know.

The horses were turning toward the stockade, and Paul frowned as he noticed the increase in activity. Troopers were talking in groups; others were going sullenly about their jobs. As the wagon lumbered through the gate, Paul greeted the sentry and warped the team into the hay yard. While he waited for Mc-

TWISTED TRAILS 101

Cune to check him in, he saw a freighter unloading some miscellaneous supplies. Two sentries, fully armed, flanked the wagon. Paul tried to puzzle this out as he watched two other men examining everything being unloaded from the big freight wagon.

When McCune came over with the stub of a cigar in his mouth and his hat shading his eyes, Paul asked, "What's all this about, Sergeant? New regulations?"

"Major Hornaby's orders, Scott. It won't delay you very much longer," McCune said with more of a military bearing than he had previously assumed.

"What does he have—visions?" Paul grinned. "Shall I back up to the stack so the load can be pulled off?"

"No; pull up alongside this morning. We're unloading by hand," McCune answered.

Paul's curiosity was aroused.

"What are you looking for?" he asked.

"Booze. The major took one of his sneak walks at sunup and found the sentry on Post One asleep drunk. He had men search the camp to find where the booze was coming from. One of the three bottles they found was in his quarters. Some joker managed to take the bottle out of my hut and plant it on the major. Nobody would confess, and that made Hornaby madder than ever. He says he's going to find the bootleggers and crack down on them."

Paul laughed shortly. "You're going to be wasting

a lot of energy searching my load. I pitched that hay on myself."

McCune shrugged. "That may be true, but my men need the exercise."

The freight wagon, its end-gate banging and the chains dragging on the ground, lumbered away, and the two armed men approached as Paul drove the team alongside the stack. Two scowling troopers with pitchforks climbed the load and began methodically to fork the hay onto the stack.

Indifferent to the hay pitchers, Paul climbed to the ground and spoke to McCune.

"Hey, Sergeant, you or your men didn't see Bighead Larson riding this way right after dark last night, did you?"

McCune answered very carefully, "No, I didn't see him riding around here. Why do you ask?"

"I had some trouble with him last night, and he got away from me."

From behind Paul came Hornaby's clipped voice.

"What sort of trouble did you have with him, Mr. Scott?" the major inquired.

"He tried to kill me," Paul said bluntly.

"With a rifle?"

Hornaby had come around and was looking Paul straight in the eye now. The major's face wore a mocking expression.

"Yes, with a rifle," Paul admitted.

TWISTED TRAILS

"And he missed you?"

"That's apparent, isn't it?" Paul couldn't keep the scorn out of his voice.

"Have you ever seen Big-head Larson shoot a rifle?"

"Yes, but I happened to move, and he missed me."

Just then there was the distinct clink of metal against glass. Hornaby smiled without humor. "All right, men. Pull the hay apart and take it out."

Paul felt a hot flush warm him. Hornaby had never liked him, and he had never cared much for the major. Now Hornaby's manner was both insulting and triumphant. Unable to believe his eyes, Paul saw the two men on the load fish four bottles of whiskey from the hay.

"What do you say to that, Mr. Scott?" Hornaby asked with pure malice in his eyes.

Paul could find no immediate answer, because the whole frame-up was so preposterous. He had the feeling of a man in a nightmare. Again he thought of Alonzo Finch and of the man who had been prowling about the barn the night before.

"What do *you* make of it, Major?" Paul countered lamely.

"It's obvious," Hornaby snapped. "Don't tell me you didn't know the whiskey was there. This isn't the first whiskey you've brought in, I'm sure of that."

"Frankly," Paul said, calming down, "I didn't

know it was there."

"I overheard you say you loaded the hay yourself."

"That's right. But the bottles could have been shoved under the hay with a forked stick after it was loaded."

"I can't quite accept that. I'm looking for a whiskey smuggler. I catch you with the goods. Why should I look further?"

"Because, confound you," Paul gritted, "I'm no smuggler. This is a frame-up, and you're in on the frame."

"That I must deny," Hornaby said shortly.

"Then how did you know the booze was there?"

"I was in receipt of certain information, and I acted upon it. The information has proved correct. I must place you under arrest, Mr. Scott."

"Major," Paul said quietly, "it's obvious why you're out here in command of this rag-tag outfit. You've got no judgment. I'm afraid you'll find there is no law against whiskey in this territory. The rules you make for your men do not apply to civilians."

"Smuggling to the Indians is against the law. Sergeant," he turned to McCune, "place this man under arrest."

McCune said, "How about confining him to my quarters, sir? The guardhouse is probably crawling with vermin from those graves we had there last night."

Hornaby's mouth was tight and pinched. "Take him to my office. We'll continue the investigation there. And don't discuss the matter with the prisoner, understand?"

McCune shrugged. "Yes, sir." Aside he said, "I got to give you credit, Major. You sure do make it hard on yourself."

As they walked through the dust to the major's office, located at the front of his quarters and connected directly with them, Paul felt foolish. He realized that the major had to do something to uphold discipline on the post, but jailing a civilian for selling whiskey was making a mountain out of a molehill. Hornaby appeared too intelligent to go to all that trouble for such an offense. His proper action would have been to forbid Paul admission to the post, or refuse to buy more fodder from Uriah. A little worry stirred lazily in Paul's mind.

"McCune, what do you make of all this?" Paul asked.

McCune broke the ash off his cigar and began to chew the short butt. "Just take it easy. Give him rope —give him rope. I think I know what's on his mind. Let's see what he does with it."

They turned from the bright sunshine into the dim office, and the smell of dust, leather and horses came in with them. The major took his seat behind the rough pine table that served as a desk. On the unpainted board wall that divided the office from Hornaby's quarters hung a crude map of the valley. The army post was marked with a circle, and new pencil marks surrounded it to end in a heavy cross. Once in the office, Paul felt his uneasiness increase. There was more there than met the eye.

"You may sit down if you wish, Mr. Scott," Hornaby said.

"Thanks; I'll stand. This business can't take more than a few minutes."

"I am afraid it's going to take much longer."

"What do you mean?"

There was a bright, eager look in the major's eyes.

"How long have you been smuggling whiskey to the camp?"

"I told you I haven't smuggled any whiskey to the camp."

"How much whiskey have you smuggled to the Indians?"

"None. None. None."

"We had three drunken braves in here last night. Somebody sold them whiskey, or else they stole it. Addie wouldn't sell them any. If they had stolen it from her, I would have heard of it."

Paul asked, his eyes puckered in a frown, "Who told you that whiskey was in my load of hay?"

"I received a note."

"From whom? Come on; name names."

"It was unsigned, but it proved to be accurate," Hornaby said.

Paul hesitated. Nobody would be allowed to enter the post during the night, but somebody must have bribed the sentry to pass a note along. The men of the post were interested in finding the bootlegger in order to end their confinement to the post. Stebbins and Miles hated his guts. But none of it made sense. There was nothing here to prove how the Indians got their whiskey, and Paul himself had broken no law.

"Look, Major," Paul said patiently, "this is getting you nowhere. You have no proof that I supplied the Indians with liquor. As far as the liquor in the hay goes, I broke your rules, but I didn't break any law. You've got nothing to hold me for."

The eager light in Hornaby's eyes sharpened. "Maybe not, Mr. Scott. Would you mind coming with me for a moment? I've got something to show you."

More to satisfy his growing curiosity than to humor the major, Paul consented. He followed Hornaby down the row of huts to the infirmary, and entered the low, evil-smelling room. Inside, he stood for a moment, unable to believe what he saw. There was the body of Big-head Larson, his face still slightly bruised from the cuffing Paul had given him, and a small blossom of blood at his throat. For a moment a dreadful feeling came over Paul. Big-head was dead

—had been dead, apparently, for hours. Paul recalled how he had held his knife at Big-head's throat the night before. Then he suddenly remembered that he had forgotten to find his knife and take it with him when he had crawled out of Big-head's room.

Paul knew the color had drained from his face, but he looked Hornaby defiantly in the eye.

"Where did you find him? What happened to him?" he asked.

"Now," Hornaby said smoothly, "shall we go back to my office and continue the investigation?"

Back in Hornaby's office, Paul repeated his questions.

"He was found out in the brush this morning. Right here." The major rose and pointed to the cross on the map. "There was an arrow sticking in his back," Hornaby told him.

"Well, why hold me? I'm no Indian," Paul said.

"But he wasn't killed with an arrow," Hornaby went on with a sly grin. "He was killed with a knife which had been twisted to enlarge the wound, and the arrow had been stuck into the wound after Big-head was dead."

"And you're accusing me of that?" Paul demanded.

"I'm not accusing anybody yet," Hornaby said. "There are some things, however, that I'd like you to explain."

TWISTED TRAILS 109

With that Hornaby rose, went to the door opening into his quarters, and said, "All right; you can come out now."

He stood politely aside, and Gladys entered the room, her eyes shrewd and her lips tight. The smell of cheap perfume preceded her like a banner.

When Norah awoke, she lay savoring the strange, new feeling of having entered a different, mysterious existence. She recalled, with a small guilty smile, how late she and Paul had remained in the kitchen the night before. With the lamp turned low, they had sat there making small talk as though by mutual agreement they avoided what they most wanted to say.

Suddenly she remembered Uriah had brought home a letter for Paul and had given it to her. How could she have forgotten it?

She found her jacket where Uriah had placed it, across the back of a chair. Quickly she searched the pocket and then stopped, puzzled. The letter was gone! Her mind leaped to her mother, who wanted to interest her in Alonzo. But she doubted her mother would open anybody's mail. It was more probable that she had lost the letter the night before when she was helping Uriah chase the interloper in the barnyard. She must go look for it at once.

But the letter was not to be found. Norah retraced her steps about the yard, looked through the loose hay near the stack, even went inside the barn, though she did not remember entering the barn the night before. What was she to do? The letter might have had an important bearing on Paul's mission there, and now it was gone. How could she tell him?

She went into the bunkhouse, hoping the letter might be there, but she did not see it on the table or on the shelf over the bunks. Aaron appeared to be sleeping, his breath a wheezy sound. The remains of the breakfast the Indian girl had brought him lay on a tray near his bunk. Unconsciously, Norah's hand smoothed Paul's bunk as she stood there thinking. Then something caught her eye under the head of Eglund's bunk. It glowed dully in the meager light from the window.

She picked up the gold piece, turning it over. How had it come there? She saw the disarrayed straw under the edge of the blanket. Slipping her hand into the straw, she drew out four more gold pieces. Uriah never paid Egg in gold pieces; in fact, after Egg's board and tobacco were paid for, there was usually only a handful of silver left. Egg was being paid for something beside his regular job. Maybe it hadn't been Big-head who had fired the bullet the night before. Big-head might have been only a decoy.

Tossing the gold in full view on top of the blanket, she picked up the breakfast tray and went out. Let Eglund worry for a while. It might be easier to get him to talk. It was hard to visualize Eglund as a bushwhacker. The money might be gambling winnings.

Back in the kitchen, her mother was waiting for her; breakfast was ready on the table.

Norah had finished eating when the bang and clatter of the hayrack came from the yard. Paul was returning. She felt a quickening of her pulse. Would there still exist between them the intimacy of feeling she had experienced last night? She thought of the letter, and the thought put a damper on her spirits. How could she tell him that the letter had been lost? Of course he would suggest a further search for it, but where?"

Quickly she got up and hurried outside, conscious of her mother's calculating eyes upon her. She ran from the porch toward the stack yard, her eagerness increasing with every step. She felt the warm color in her face, and tried to smooth it away with her hand. But what difference did it make? She had already confessed her love to him. What more was there to say or do?

A man came around the hayrack, but it wasn't Paul. It was a trooper from the post. Norah felt a chill hand grip her heart.

"Where's Mr. Scott?" she asked in a stilted voice.

"I reckon, ma'am, he's bein' detained by the major."

"He's not hurt—he's all right?"

"So far he's all right," the trooper said.

"What do you mean by that? What happened? Come on; tell me," Norah said quickly.

"I ain't got much to tell, ma'am. Major Hornaby found whiskey in the load of hay. A man was killed in the brush last night. I reckon the major's lookin' for somebody to pin the murder on."

"Not Paul!"

"The sergeant told me to drive this here team back, ma'am. I got my horse tied on the other side of the wagon. Good day to you, ma'am."

Norah didn't wait to reply to the man. She rushed into the barn to get her horse. Her hands fumbled with the bridle; then the smooth, inquiring voice of Alonzo Finch was at her shoulder.

"Are you going some place?"

"A man has been murdered near the post, and Major Hornaby's holding Paul."

"Well, now, just a minute," Alonzo said. "I came here for lunch at the invitation of your mother, who thought it would be nice for us all to go buggy riding."

"My mother will entertain you, Alonzo. I've got to go to Paul."

"Naturally," he agreed, taking the bridle from her and slipping it over the horse's head. "I think Helen will excuse me. I had better go along with you."

"I'd rather go alone," Norah said.

Alonzo swung her saddle to the horse's back and

reached for the cinch. "Oh, no, my dear. I might be of help to you," Finch said.

Paul stared at Gladys as she emerged from Hornaby's quarters and recognized her as the girl he had seen at the door of her room the night before.

"All right, Miss Gladys," the major said, "you sit right over there."

Dr. Cranny came in, a little steadier than usual. His small eyes were bright and furtive, but his voice had a new, deep quality in it.

"You'll want me in on this, Major, I presume?" he asked, sitting in a corner.

Paul looked about him and felt as though the walls were moving in to crush him.

Hornaby said, "You might as well sit down, Scott. This may take some time."

Paul said impatiently, "It's taken too much time already. If you expect to prove anything against me, you're wasting your time. I can account for my actions last night."

"All right, Mr. Scott, account for your time," Hornaby said. "Tell us just what you did last night."

"I was shot at last night in the orchard at the Young house. I happened to move just when the shot was fired, or I would be dead. I cut out after the bushwhacker, but he got away. I figured he went to Addie's. I found Big-head in bed with his clothes on and still damp from perspiration. I tried to make him confess who had hired him to kill me, but he refused, and I struck him. Then he got a foot free of the covers and rammed it into my stomach. I fell back against the commode and got knocked out. When I came to, Big-head was gone," Paul said simply.

"That's all that happened?" Hornaby asked.

"I reckon so."

"Did you cover that booze with hay before or after you were shot at?" Hornaby asked quickly.

"I didn't cover any booze with hay, and I didn't kill Larson."

There was a disturbance, and Stebbins and Miles crowded into the small room.

Hornaby turned from Paul and addressed Gladys. "Miss Gladys, will you tell us just why you came to see me this morning?"

"Well, I heard at the Lone Chance that Big-head had been killed, and I thought I might help find out who killed him."

"At what time did you hear the news?"

"I don't get up early as a rule, but I was restless because of something that happened last night. I guess I heard it about eight o'clock," Gladys said with the air of one trying to be very precise.

"Who brought the news?"

"Eglund, the guy who works for Uriah Young."

"When you heard that Big-head was dead, you became suspicious of something that happened last night, and decided to come here and tell me?" Hornaby asked.

"That's right."

"Tell us what it was that disturbed you last night."

"Well, I don't want to get anybody in bad trouble," she looked at Paul, "but Mr. Scott came to my room last night."

"I stopped at your door," Paul corrected her.

She cast him a venomous look. "He asked me if I'd heard a man come up the stairs just before that. I told him no. Later I heard a noise and looked out into the hall. Big-head's room is at the end of the hall, and the noise was coming from there. There was quite a loud thump, and right after, Big-head went past my door in a hurry, and I saw some blood dripping off his face or neck. Mr. Scott never came by, so later I went to Big-head's room and lit the candle there. Nobody was there. I found a bloody knife on the floor, and that was all."

Paul cursed himself for having left the knife behind. He watched the major and saw him reach across the table and very dramatically uncover the long-bladed stock knife.

"Mr. Scott, have you ever seen this knife before?" Hornaby asked pompously.

"Of course I have. It's my knife."

"And how did it get into Larson's room? How did

it come to be left there, opened and bloody?"

"To try to scare Larson into talking, I held my knife at his throat, but I didn't stab him. When he kicked me in the stomach, the knife might have stuck him slightly in the throat. You saw the wound; it wasn't enough to kill him."

Hornaby turned as though to disregard that statement. He said, "Mr. Stebbins, you and Mr. Miles were with the patrol that found the body. Can you tell us about it?"

Stebbins licked his lips and looked at Miles. He rose awkwardly, and his long pendulous jaw moved for a moment before he spoke.

"We found the dead man, sir, just like the lieutenant told McCune. There was an arrow in his back, but even the lieutenant could see—"

"What do you mean 'even' the lieutenant, Mr. Stebbins?" Hornaby inquired.

Stebbins' long face flushed.

"I mean Lieutenant Skaggs saw right away the arrow didn't kill him. It was stickin' in his back all right, but the hole looked like it had been made with a knife and then the arrow punched in later to make it look like Indians done the job."

Paul turned on Stebbins and said, "If you intend to lie, Stebbins, then lie, but don't spout all this second-hand garbage that's been put in your mind."

Hornaby snapped, "I'll run this investigation, Mr.

Scott."

"Look, Major," Paul retorted, "I'm not going to sit here and be pushed around. This isn't a court of law, and nobody's under oath. You're going about this like a man who'd like to see a lynching. You know Miles and Stebbins hate my guts. What authority on the character of wounds are they?"

"All right," Hornaby said agreeably; "we'll get expert testimony. Dr. Cranny, will you give us your opinion on how Larson died?"

Cranny stood up, harrumphing to clear his throat. A blast of liquor-laden air came from his thick lips and filled the room. Somebody opened the door wide to let in more air.

"The deceased came to his end from a stab wound in the back. An arrow had been thrust into the wound after death. This was evident by the nature of the wound and the condition of the arrowhead. If the man had been killed by an arrow, the blood would have been clotted thickly about the arrowhead, and also would have run back along the shaft of the arrow."

"At what time would you say the crime had been committed?" Hornaby asked, leaning forward over the table.

"I examined the body around eight o'clock this morning. In my opinion, judging from the condition of the deceased, the crime had been committed about midnight."

Paul did not see Norah and Finch arrive. He was watching the doctor, and the next time he switched his eyes to the door, Norah and Finch were standing in the opening. Norah's eyes were wide as she listened intently to the doctor's testimony.

"Could you, Doctor, describe the kind of knife that would make such a wound?" Hornaby asked.

"That would be difficult. The knife had been twisted, and the wound was enlarged by the arrowhead."

"Could a knife such as this have killed Larson?" The major held up Paul's knife.

"It would be possible if the blade was driven in all the way."

"Could you give us any kind of an analysis which would prove that the blood on this knife and the blood of Larson are one and the same?"

Paul broke in fiercely, "Of course it's the same. You don't need an analysis. I've told you what happened. If that stock knife killed Larson, there'd be blood all over it, even on the handle."

"Perhaps." Hornaby nodded. "Some of it could have been wiped off."

"Larson couldn't have run from his room out into the brush with such a wound in his back, you know that."

"Who said he did? Who said you killed him in his room? You haven't explained just where you were

TWISTED TRAILS 119

at midnight last night."

Here it was, the question Paul wanted to avoid. Decent people seldom remained up until after midnight. Norah was a girl, a young, desirable girl, and for her to keep such hours with a man—well, Paul could imagine how Stebbins or Miles or even Gladys could tell about it with sly smirks.

"I was in my bunk asleep," Paul said.

"How can you prove that?" Hornaby insisted. "You admitted you were after Larson, that you assaulted him. What was to keep you from following him out into the brush and killing him?"

Norah's voice from the doorway, clear and firm, caused every head to turn. Her chin was up and her hazel eyes blazing.

"I was with Paul when he was shot at, Major," she said evenly. "I met him when he came back from the Lone Chance. That was early, about eight o'clock. He had left without supper, so I fixed him something to eat. He was with me in the kitchen until midnight or after!" she finished defiantly.

There was a murmur in the room, and eyes took on sly, calculating expressions. Major Hornaby looked around with a smug expression and turned his eyes back to Norah.

"And what, may I ask, were you two doing there all that time?"

Paul felt anger explode in him. He covered the

floor in two steps, his face white and set. His long body bent over the table, and he slapped Hornaby across the teeth.

"Major," he cried, "that's no affair of yours!"

Hornaby froze in his chair, fire flooding his lean face. It was as though he had turned to stone. Paul's eyes pinioned him, and Paul saw the man's immense pride fighting his vacillating courage. At last Hornaby's hand moved and picked up a pencil. He scribbled on a piece of paper and shoved it toward Paul. Without reading it, Paul shoved the paper into his pocket.

"You came here, Mr. Scott," Hornaby said, "with a bad reputation."

"What do you know about my reputation? You've listened to Alonzo Finch mouth his lies."

"I haven't heard you deny them."

Then Finch was pushing in through the doorway, a cocksure twist to his lips and an eager light in his eyes.

"Can you deny, Paul, that your brother Pete was lynched for murder?"

"You helped lead the mob that lynched him, Finch," Paul said accusingly. "He was lynched, but he was no murderer. He died in another man's place."

"And Larry wasn't run out of town?"

"Look, my brothers got in bad company, I'll admit that. It's useless for me to declare that you were the

TWISTED TRAILS 121

one who badgered them into what crimes they committed. Let's tell it all. I'm a crook in the minds of my friends and neighbors back home, sure, but I was framed, and I've come here to take back the man who is guilty."

There was a jumble of voices in the room until Major Hornaby slapped on the table for order.

"Mr. Scott, you're a disturbing influence here. You spawn trouble."

"Major, I think you'll find most of that trouble stems from the same source."

"Why don't you take your man and go home?"

"Because I am going to do it legal, and that takes time—not like this kangaroo court of yours."

Hornaby slumped as though some of the starch had gone out of him.

"Everybody clear out of here but Mr. Scott," he ordered. "Go on; get out and close the door. Stebbins, get them out and keep them out."

When the room was quiet once more, Major Hornaby spoke, keeping his eyes on the table.

"It's going to take a lot more evidence than I have to stick this murder on anybody. You had a motive, but Norah's testimony is in your favor. If you feel I insulted her in any way, I'm sorry, but I don't like being slapped in public. My advice to you is to get out of the valley, Scott."

"When I go, Finch goes with me."

Hornaby shook his head. "You stay around here at your own risk, Scott. I don't want you to set foot on the post again and shall give orders to that effect. I'm of the opinion that Finch will either kill you or get out of the country before your warrant arrives. You're free to go."

"Do me a favor, Major," Scott said. "In a way it's your duty. Send the doctor to see Sodek. It was your men who laid him low."

"That much I can do," Hornaby said.

Scott left without another word. He had to find Norah. But when he arrived at the gate, he was told that Norah had ridden away with Finch.

A trooper rode up, leading a saddled horse which he turned over to Paul.

"The major says to loan you a mount, mister. We'll pick it up at the ranch later."

Chapter 7

Accepting the loan of a horse from the trooper, Paul was about to mount when Sergeant McCune tapped him on the shoulder. Some of the stiffness had gone out of McCune, and he wore a friendly grin.

"The major's had his fun; you'd better stay and have mess with us. It's late."

"I've been ordered off the post, with instructions to stay off. Don't you think I'd better travel?" Paul asked.

"You're not off the post yet. Come on; eat with me. Hornaby won't dare say anything; he's made enough of an ass of himself," McCune urged.

"He does have a murder to solve," Paul reminded him.

"Yeah, but there's darned little solvin' he can do sitting on his rump in an office. If he catches the murderer, somebody else will have to stake the man out for him."

Paul yielded to the invitation and followed Mc-

Cune into the mess shack. The troopers gave him a curious once-over and forgot him. Hornaby was not there, as he usually had a light lunch brought to his quarters.

As he ate the savory beans, pork and turnips, washed down with great gulps of coffee, Paul asked:

"Just where was Larson killed, Mac?"

"About two miles southwest of the post, near as I could make out. That's toward the Indian village, but not in a direct line with it. You saw the cross on the map," McCune said.

Mess over, Paul said, "Thanks for everything, Mac." He mounted the borrowed horse, but instead of heading toward the ranch, he turned down into the valley. It was not difficult to follow the trail left by the morning patrol, but when Paul reached the place where Big-head had been found, he discovered a disheartening confusion of tracks. The ground was pounded and scored with them. Patiently, Paul attempted to unravel the tracks and isolate those of the dead man and his murderer.

He finally found the trail he was looking for. Out of the confusion of hoof prints, he traced one horse without shoes, which was undoubtedly Indian, and one with a peculiarly narrow shoe. Eventually the tracks led beyond Lieutenant Skaggs' and traveled on alone. It had taken a long time on foot to find what he wanted, but now he mounted.

Riding carefully to one side of the tracks he followed, Paul came to the place where the two tracks had joined. He followed the Indian tracks until he was convinced they had come from the Indian village. Then he backtracked the horse with the narrow shoes until it was evident that it had come from the direction of the Lone Chance. The horse had not traveled fast, he could tell that. Who had been on that horse, riding to the fatal spot where Big-head had been found and murdered?

He didn't stay with the trail. There were gullies there, cutbacks that could hide and protect a man. If the killer found him following a trail, he might make another, successful attempt to kill him. He felt the weight of Big-head's purse in his pocket. He had forgotten he had it until now. He took it out and, opening it, counted the five gold pieces it contained.

The price of a life, he thought, my life. This could be but a down payment. A bought killer is a continual menace. He can go on bleeding his buyer for life in payment for silence. Gladys had testified that Big-head had run down the stairs and through the saloon. The man who had paid him to do murder could have seen him and realized suddenly that Big-head might be forced to talk. Therefore the man must have followed Big-head and killed him. But the tracks of the Indian pony clouded the issue. There had been drunken Indians last night.

Paul saw the ranch just ahead of him, and as he rode into the yard, he looked about eagerly, hoping Norah would be there. Then he saw that the buggy was gone. So Norah had gone with Finch again, even after declaring her love. Had Finch's re-iteration of the charges against him made her regret her declaration?

Paul went into the barn and saddled his own horse. Then he went to the bunkhouse to roll up his blankets. He stopped in the middle of the floor, a perplexed frown furrowing his forehead. Five gold coins lay yellow and gleaming on Eglund's bunk. How had they come there? Why? Had they been put there in plain sight as a warning to him?

Paul picked up a sack of makings from the shelf over his bunk and stuffed them into his pocket. Not until then did he remember the note Major Hornaby had scribbled and handed him during the kangaroo court trial. Now he pulled out the note, and read:

> *I'll be in back of the stables tonight after retreat. We'll see how well you can use your hands then.*

Paul's lips formed a tight, straight line. Another fight. How many more fights would it take before they let him alone? He tore the note up into little pieces and threw them out the window. Then he picked up his blanket roll and went outside. The

TWISTED TRAILS 127

house was quiet. He supposed Helen was napping, and he didn't much care to face her just then. Fastening his bedroll to his saddle, he mounted his horse and, leading the army horse, headed for the trading post.

The low-ceilinged trading post smelled of bacon and hides, coffee and spices. Flour made a white pyramid in the middle of the floor. There were beans in an open sack, and brown, raw sugar. Smoked meat hung from hooks suspended from the ceiling, and on one side, in back of a plank counter, there was a gaudy array of cloth. Paul found Uriah working over his ledger at a high counter in the rear.

"What's the trouble, son?" Uriah asked, looking over the glasses he wore only for accounting.

"Uriah," Paul began slowly, feeling for words, "I've had nothing but trouble since I got here."

"I wouldn't say that. What trouble you did have, you handled right smart. If you think you'd rather take a ridin' job, back in the hills—"

"No, it isn't that. I can't leave here, because if I did Finch would get away from me again. I spent too much time hunting for him to let him slip out now. It can't take much more time for the marshal to arrive with the warrant I sent for. Reckon I'll make out all right."

"Did Norah give you the letter that came in the mail yesterday?" Uriah asked.

Paul thought he had not heard right. "What did you say?"

"I said, did Norah give you the letter that came in the mail for you?"

"A letter? She didn't mention it. Are you sure she had it?"

Paul saw a curious expression come over Uriah's face.

"I gave it to her. She put it in the pocket of her jacket. I reckon she must've forgot to give it to you. Don't make much sense, though. With mail as scarce as it is, ain't likely anybody would forget a letter."

"That shot frightened her," Paul said, trying to find an explanation. He was disturbed, too. There had been plenty of time for her to tell him about a letter when they were sitting up the night before.

"I didn't give the letter to her until after the shot. I wasn't home then. Reckon I could've taken care—"

"She could have forgotten," Paul said, trying not to sound dubious. "Tell her I'll come down in the morning for it."

"What's wrong with tonight at supper?" Uriah asked, his gray eyes questing.

"I'm quitting my job, Uriah," Paul said. He went on to explain how Hornaby had ruled him off the post. "If I can't enter the post, I can't deliver hay. It's that simple. Hornaby would still like to pin the murder on me."

TWISTED TRAILS

"Look," Uriah said, his craggy face pleading, "I like you—like you a lot, Paul. Work for me here at the store."

The older man's friendship warmed Paul.

"I'd rather not say right now, Uriah," Paul told him. "There's two or three things I want to get settled."

"Such as?"

"For one thing, I'm going to try and find out who paid Big-head to shoot at me. Maybe it was Finch; maybe it wasn't. I have other enemies here, and, knowing about my reason for being here and the quarrel between Finch and me, they might figure they can get away with murder and let Finch take the blame."

"If I can help you in any way, let me know," Uriah offered.

"Thanks, Uriah. Tell me something. Where would Eglund come on five gold pieces?" Paul asked.

Uriah rubbed his graying hair across his head and said, "I reckon he's got a sideline. I ain't a man to interfere in other people's business, so long as they leave me alone. Eglund, backed by another party, is smuggling whiskey where it ain't wanted."

"Who's back of him? Finch?"

"Nope. He was doing it before Finch came here."

"Addie?"

"I reckon Addie ain't after that kind of money.

Neither am I, in case you're thinking of asking me."

Paul showed Big-head's purse. "Big-head got five double eagles, too. I reckon the coyote who's back of all this has a fixed price for anything: a hundred bucks flat rate for bullets or booze."

"Might be no connection," Uriah grunted. "I'll see what I can worm outa Eglund. He's right simple once you know how he ticks."

It was getting on into the afternoon. "I've got to go now," Paul said without explanation. Then, thinking of the coming meeting with Hornaby, he added with a grin, "I may be back for some arnica later on."

When Paul entered the Lone Chance dining room the evening rush was over, and he felt a lift as he saw Addie hurrying toward him from the door leading into the saloon. He had washed the blood off his face, but it was still cut and sore, and he saw hurt and dismay come into Addie's eyes when she noticed this.

"Paul—another fight?" she asked softly as she followed him to the rear of the room and sat across from him at a table.

"This was an affair of honor, Addie," he said, and grinned at her.

"You talk as if you'd had a duel."

"I did, sort of. Hornaby made a remark this morning when he was questioning me, and I didn't like it. I slapped him across the mouth, and he invited me out back of the stables after retreat."

"You mean to tell me Hornaby did that after the way you beat up Stebbins and Miles?"

"Oh, he's not really a coward," Paul said; "he just don't know when to be brave." Then he added, "I'm starved, Addie. How about some dinner?"

"Didn't you eat at the Youngs'?"

"I don't live there or work there any more."

Because the girls were through in the dining room and were out in the bar by now, Addie went to the kitchen and ordered food for Paul. When she came back, she said:

"Tell me about the fight."

Paul shrugged. "There isn't much to tell. The major's a good man with his fists—scientific," Paul said, rubbing his jaw reflectively. "He knocked me down a couple of times. That scientific fighting can tire a man out. Too much traveling."

"What did you do to him? You act as though you enjoyed the fight," Addie said.

"Could be," he acknowledged. "Let's say the fight ended in a draw. Leastways, I think the major and I understand each other better now."

The food came, and as he ate, Addie talked to him.

"What are you going to do now, Paul?"

"I'm not sure."

"You going to cut and run without Alonzo?"

"Look, Addie, I've been framed, kicked around, shot at. I've got only a few more days to wait, and I intend to wait. If I live that long, Finch is going back with me."

"In the meantime, what are you going to do?"

"I figured maybe you had a room here for me— I'll just hang around and wait for the warrant." He remembered the letter he had not received and frowned.

"I'm glad you quit your job," Addie said.

"Why?" Paul asked suspiciously. "Why should you be glad?"

"Carmody, Farrow and myself intend to offer you a proposition. They're coming over tonight."

"What kind of proposition could you offer me, Addie? I'm suspected of murder, branded a thief. . . ."

"I think I know who the murderer is," Addie said softly, a note of sadness creeping into her voice.

"Well, for gosh sakes, speak up!"

"Not yet, Paul. I want to be sure. If we pick the wrong man, the right man will go free. When you're through eating, come up to my room." With that, Addie rose and went through the bar and up the stairway.

Paul went into the bar and saw Alonzo Finch

TWISTED TRAILS 133

drinking at the bar with a couple of miners.

Paul sauntered up to the bar, caught Finch's attention and said, "How about drinks all around?"

The miners looked at Paul with respect and friendliness. "We sure would be proud to drink with you, Scott."

"Does hay hauling pay so well that you can afford to treat, Paul?" Finch asked.

"It doesn't pay as well as some other things, Finch," Paul replied. He took out Big-head's purse and tossed it on the bar in full view of Finch.

"Where did you get that?" Finch said, the slightest hesitation in his guarded voice.

"Do you recognize it, Alonzo? I took it off Big-head Larson."

"But I thought you said you didn't kill him."

"I didn't. But you know what I think, Finch? I think you paid him what's in that purse to kill me!"

The miners moved uneasily. Finch, though his gun was hidden, was armed, and Paul wore his forty-five in full view on his hip.

"Paul, you're still a nuisance. One of these days you're going to find yourself in trouble," Finch said evenly. His soft-looking body appeared to harden and grow taller.

"How about now?" Paul asked, pushing back from the bar.

Finch shrugged. "Why should I do the law's

work?"

Addie appeared at the foot of the stairs and beckoned to Paul. He picked up the purse that had belonged to Big-head, threw a coin on the bar and told the others to order up. Then he turned to follow Addie to her room.

For a moment he felt uncomfortable and out of place in the luxuriously furnished room, that smelled of perfume and cosmetics. Candles shed a soft radiance upon the silk bedspread and the brocade furniture.

"You've got a right pretty place here, Addie," Paul complimented her.

"I've got some good brandy, too," she said. "That stuff at the bar isn't much good, but it's all I can get here. I have this sent out from New York."

She poured him a small glass of the amber fluid. Her every movement was graceful and yet dead sure. Paul sipped the brandy and felt it burn in his stomach.

"Why did you want me here, Addie?" he asked, watching her.

"Don't you like it?"

"I reckon it's real nice—too nice for a rough man in a rough country to appreciate. It would soften him."

"A man like you can get too hard, Paul."

"I wouldn't know. I know only that somebody is

bent on making it tough for me. They're willing to go to any extreme except meeting me face to face. That meeting's got to come, and I can't afford to be soft about it, Addie."

"I was gauging you," she said with ill-concealed pleasure. "We want to hire you as a man to keep the law here. . . ."

Before Paul could reply, there was the scrape of feet in the hall, and Addie let Carmody and Farrow into the room. These men, too, felt uneasy in such feminine surroundings. Addie poured them all drinks and invited the men to sit. Carmody was a typical railroad man, broad of chest, thick of arm. His hands were huge, and the whiskey glass appeared fragile and helpless in his grasp. Farrow was different, a tall, rawhide man of loose construction. His face wore the pallor of the mines, and his eyes were squinted, but at home, in the candlelight.

"You do the talking, Addie," Carmody said gruffly.

"There's not much talking to do. This camp is going to start booming like a mushroom once things get started. We're the people in on the ground floor, and if we keep a tight grip, the town will run our way. You've proved yourself here, Paul, as a man who can fight and isn't afraid. We want to hire you to keep things honest and quiet."

Paul looked about at the serious faces and felt

flattered by the offer. "Look here," he said. "Even if I agreed to accept your offer, it wouldn't stick. You couldn't just hand me a lawman's job. I'd have to be appointed. . . ."

"That would come. Right now we need you," Carmody put in earnestly. "Day after tomorrow I've got the payroll coming in. It was stolen once right off the stage."

Farrow, his voice a little wheezy, said, "We've hit a vein of gold up on the hill; danged near pure metal. I've got a special crew mining that gold, men I can trust. But if rumor gets out that I'm holding that kind of stuff, it will be stolen before I can get it to Salt Lake. We can tell folks hereabouts that you were deputized by mail. When the marshal comes, he can do it proper."

"I hope to have him do it proper," Paul agreed, "but just so I can take Finch back to Oklahoma with me. You see I won't be here long enough to do much good."

"Why don't you try it, Paul?" Addie said. "It might give you a chance to find Big-head's killer. Much might happen before you leave here."

"Look, Addie, the warrant I'm waiting for might be here day after tomorrow."

"Will you take a special job?" Carmody asked, then, his big hands fondling the empty whiskey glass.

"Doing exactly what?"

TWISTED TRAILS

Carmody looked around as though making sure nobody outside the room could hear. "I want you to ride out and meet the stagecoach when it comes in, and act as a special guard."

"Don't they carry a guard?"

"Sure, but I want to make it look good. It's just for looks, to keep 'em guessing."

"How do you mean that?"

Carmody grinned, his big, round face lighting up slyly. "The payroll won't be on the stage. This is a secret between us here. Addie knows about it, and so does Farrow. We've all used the same trick now and then. The payroll money is coming with an old trapper in a dilapidated buckboard. It's a hardscrabble outfit nobody would suspect was worth thirty cents. We've banking on him getting through, but to make it look right, I want the extra guard on the stage. Do you savvy?"

"I savvy all right, Mr. Carmody, but I'm not sure I want to get shot up guarding something that isn't there."

"You don't have to carry it as far as bullets. Besides, the mail will be on the coach. It might carry the warrant you're wantin' so bad."

"Things are getting worse here lately," Addie took up the argument. "I don't like men being shot at, I don't like murder. We'll hire you as a sort of special agent until we see how it works out. Grievy was

once a deputy, and I've still got his star. What do
you say, Paul?"

"Keep your star, Addie," he said, and saw the
accusation in her eyes. They all looked at him, judged
him, and thought he was afraid. "But I'll take the
special job, Carmody. I'll guard the stagecoach, because I've got a stake in the job myself. I want that
warrant or any other kind of orders that come through
that will give me a legal hold on Finch. Reckon,
though, the marshal from Salt Lake might bring the
warrant personally."

Addie said, disappointment in her low, husky
voice, "That's your answer, then?"

"I'm sorry, Addie," Paul said softly.

Farrow said solemnly, his pasty face grim, "I
think you're making a mistake, Scott. I don't know
what Finch did to you back in Oklahoma, but if
you're not there it can't hurt you. You're cut out
for this land, Scott. It's a growing land, and you
can grow with it. There's stuff to fight for here, and
you can fight."

"What Finch did to me in Oklahoma isn't important only to me. My folks are still alive there. They're
entitled to the respect and trust of the community.
My brothers did some bad things, but not so bad
as they were painted. I want to take Finch back and
force the truth out of him."

"Suppose he murdered Big-head," Addie said.

TWISTED TRAILS 139

"Then you could get him here in the territory for murder."

"Oklahoma has first chance at him," Paul said stubbornly. "If he has any time left, this territory can have him."

Farrow rose and stretched. "You're your own man, Scott. Don't stand in your own way." Farrow said good night to Addie and went out.

"I'll see you tomorrow," Carmody said. "The stage comes in day after tomorrow; that will give you time to make plans."

He found himself alone once more with Addie and the perfume and silk and lace.

"You can share the room off the kitchen with the night cook. It's warm there, and safe," she told him.

Thanking her, Paul went on down the stairs and outside without looking toward the bar.

When Norah awoke after a restless night, she appeared in the kitchen for breakfast dressed in her flannel shirt and buckskin pants. At sight of her, her mother's face lost its animated glow and changed to an expression of critical disapproval.

"What's the matter with you, child? Why in the world do you have to dress like that?" Helen asked.

"I intend to haul the hay to the post today, Mother."

"Don't you realize you're a grown woman? That

job isn't for you any more. It was all right to do it once in a while when you were tomboying around here, but now you need some dignity."

"I don't feel, Mother, that dignity suffers through honest labor. It's a job I can do. I feel responsible for Paul being thrown off the post."

"Eglund can do it," Helen said. "What do you think Major Hornaby will think of you, dressed like a man and doing a man's work?"

"It isn't important to me what the major thinks," Norah replied, her voice level. "As for Eglund hauling the hay, he's got too much to do already. If he hauls the hay, it means that Uriah will have to do double work."

"I thought Alonzo Finch might become interested enough in you to marry you and take you away from here. I see now that it's hopeless," Helen said.

"I don't want to go away from here," Norah said fiercely. Then, changing the subject, she asked, "Did you see the letter Uriah brought for Paul night before last?"

Busying herself over the table, where she mixed the biscuit dough, Helen hesitated a moment before answering. When she spoke, there was accusation in her voice.

"Why do you ask me about that? You took charge of it."

"Yes, I know. I'm sorry I asked you."

"Why should you be sorry?" Helen asked stubbornly. "Did you think I had taken it?"

There it was, bare and ugly and in the open, the suspicion she did not want to acknowledge.

"No, Mother. I must have lost it. I thought you might have found it," Norah said too quickly.

"Perhaps Eglund found it," Helen said coldly, "or Paul Scott himself."

Norah ate her breakfast. No, Paul had not found the letter, of that she was sure. She almost bolted her food, as though she had to rush after something that was mocking and threatening her; some monster which, if she did not contrive to capture and strangle it, would eventually destroy her.

It was mid-morning when Paul met Carmody in the Lone Chance. The big-chested contractor with his high boots and big, floppy hat looked like a dressed-up bear. From his hairy face the stump of a cigar protruded, and he was puffing smoke faster than a donkey engine going upgrade.

"Hope you ain't changed your mind about that job, Scott," he said around his cigar.

"I gave you my word," Paul said levelly.

"Farrow, up at the mine, is running into the trouble he was afraid of. Somebody's getting their fingers into the pie."

Paul frowned. He recalled Farrow's story about

the high grade gold ore. Well, Farrow would have to protect that ore himself. Paul knew that, if he started taking on that job, he'd find himself stuck there. The only other occupant of the Lone Chance at the time, besides the bartender, was Alonzo Finch. He was playing a haphazard game of solitaire, ostensibly disinterested in everyone and everything about him. But he had ears like an elephant's.

"Sorry about that," Paul said.

"But not sorry enough to do anything about it? Farrow would pay big—bigger than me."

"No," Paul said.

Without looking up, Finch said, "I heard a rumor that you're taking on some weight around here, Paul."

"Maybe it isn't just a rumor," Paul said.

"You know, Paul, sometimes stage scouts get hurt —hurt real bad, especially if they're armed. What makes you think you could ever kill a man? You've never been bloodied."

"That's right, Finch," Paul said. "I hope you're around when I have to make my first try."

"I'll probably be around before, and after. Will you?"

"That's an interesting question," Paul said, and went out on the porch to sit and watch the railroad crew far up the side of the mountain grading the roadbed for the switchback track.

TWISTED TRAILS 143

At noon he ate dinner at the Lone Chance, and Addie came to share his table, but she said little. It was as though she had said everything there was to say. There was a pensiveness about her that Paul had not seen before.

"What're you thinking, Addie?" he asked, then added quickly, "No, don't tell me if you don't want to."

"I have a strange feeling, Paul," Addie said slowly. "I can't understand it. I have a frightening sense something is going to happen, something horrible, but I don't know just who it's going to happen to."

"Didn't know you were a fortune teller, Addie." Paul smiled.

"I'm not."

"Then forget it. It's just because of the way things have been going lately: Big-head killed, me shot at—"

"Maybe that's part of it. This new job you took on for Carmody might make the killer the more determined."

"I've been thinking it over. Maybe that shot missed on purpose the other night. They might just have wanted to scare me."

"They didn't try to scare Big-head; they cut a hole in his back. Be careful, Paul."

Later in the afternoon, he went back of the Lone Chance toward the stables to check his gear. It was then he saw Norah on her pinto, still dressed in flannel and buckskin, riding toward him. She was upset, sad, her eyes were clouded with despair.

"Will you go for a ride with me, Paul?" she asked without any preliminaries.

"I'd like to, Norah," he said. "What's wrong?"

"I'll tell you as we ride," she answered without enthusiasm.

Paul saddled up quickly, realizing that whatever secret it was Norah had to tell, she wanted to divulge it at once. That it was bothering her was apparent. When he was in the saddle, she said, "Let's take the mountain trail that leads back toward the cow camp."

Paul agreed, and for the first few minutes a heavy pall of silence hung between them. They rode north toward the mountain where the railroad crews worked; after crossing a deep swale, the cow camp trail swung to the left and skirted Gull Canyon. The sun was hot and the smell of sage rose sharp and bitter from the dark bushes that lined the trail. At last Norah spoke slowly, uncertainly.

"I don't know just what you think of me, Paul," she said.

"Neither do I know what I think of you," he surprised himself by saying. "I mean there are some things that are confusing.".

"Yes, there are. For instance, that letter I had for you," she went on, her eyes on the trail.

Yes, the letter. How was she going to explain that? Paul wanted to spare her.

"What happened to it," he asked without rancor.

"That's just it. I don't know!" she said in a low, agonized voice. "I had it in the pocket of my jacket that night I brought a horse for you. But Uriah made me take his heavier coat, and he took mine back into the house. In all the excitement, I forgot the letter that night, and when I looked for it in the morning, it was gone."

She paused so long that he prodded, "Lost?"

"I thought I had lost it in the yard when Uriah and I surprised the prowler, but I looked everywhere for it. Then Big-head's murder came up, and the questioning at the post. I didn't get a chance to see you. Then you moved out without saying goodbye or anything. You saw Uriah, and he mentioned the letter, and you must have thought—"

"Of course I was curious, Noah, but I never really believed you had kept the letter. I knew there must be some mistake. If it wasn't lost, then where is it? Uriah didn't have it. Who—" Paul halted lamely. Helen was the only other one who might have appropriated it. It was not for him to accuse her.

"I know what you're thinking. I don't blame you, but I can't see why Mother would do a thing like that. Anyhow, she denied it."

"Let's not accuse her. It could have been lost. Did

you notice the postmark, where it had come from?"

"It was from Oklahoma, all right."

Paul felt a deep concern, because that letter might have been the most important thing in the world to him right now. There might be no other communication from the sheriff back home, and the letter could have contained the information necessary to get Alonzo Finch back to face trial. But the letter was gone. If the stage tomorrow carried nothing further, then what?

They were riding up a steep part of the trail now, with Norah riding ahead of him, so they could not carry on a conversation very well. The horses breathed hard at the climb, their sharp hooves edging into the soft earth. The pinion and cedar trees, scrubby and dwarfed, were giving way to real pines. The valley dropped away below them, green and gray and purple. Smoke rose from the Indian village, all but invisible to the south. The fields of the ranch were huge emeralds strung together along the stream. The army post was a blurred scar in the lighter green of the greasewood.

When they reached the flat summit of a long escarpment forming a natural lookout point, they dismounted, letting the horses' reins hang. Norah sat on a big boulder, her eyes looking into the valley; Paul stood near her.

"It's beautiful, isn't it?" he hazarded.

"Nature's always beautiful," she said vaguely. "It's man who rejects and mars nature, who destroys the beauty."

"But men are nature, too, Norah. Nobody's perfect, but every man does what he must do. Some achieve great things, others small things, but they all try— Oh," he interrupted his thought, because it sounded pompous, "I don't know how to put it. If things were different—"

"I know," she said with some bitterness. "You're trying to apologize for being the way you are. Your hate comes before your love; your pride comes before your happiness."

There was no point in arguing, so he held his tongue and watched a cloud shadow racing across the flat below. Then, looking around, he saw that his horse had strayed some distance away around the curve of the mountain, so he went quietly to catch him. When he rounded the shoulder of the mountain, he had a clear view down into Gull Canyon. Then he tensed and looked back over his shoulder. From where he was, he could just see Norah, but she could not see down into the canyon, for which he breathed a prayer of thanks. As he looked down, the line cabin was plainly visible beside the road in the canyon. Behind the cabin, hidden from the road but easily seen from that high trail, stood the Youngs' buggy, and tied to a wheel of the buggy was Finch's horse.

At first Paul couldn't quite grasp the significance of what he saw, and when he did, he had a sick, lost feeling. No one could be there at such a rendezvous with Finch except Helen Young. How safe they must feel on that little traveled road with their horses hidden. The fools!

Paul knew now the thing that was bothering Norah. He was aware of a wild, relieved feeling that was almost like drunkenness. Norah must have spurned Finch, and Finch had taken this vicious way of getting even with her. Paul realized, too, that he could not mention what he saw to Norah without increasing her shame.

Capturing his horse, Paul went quickly to the rock on which Norah still sat. She rose and stood before him, in her eyes a defeated look. Before he knew it, Paul had her in his arms, soft, yielding and compliant. His lips were on hers, hard and hungry, and he became alive to depths and heights he had not known he possessed. When the storm of passion subsided, he felt humble and unworthy.

"I'm sorry, Norah," was all he could say. He couldn't tell her how he had discovered she had spurned Finch. He couldn't divulge what he had seen in Gull Canyon. Norah knew about her mother, or suspected what was going on, but she could not defend herself.

"Never mind," she said shortly. "You've made

your try and found out what you could do. You'll be gone in a day or two, or you'll be dead."

Paul said, "What do you mean by that? It sounds sinister."

"Finch is an evil man—more evil than a gunman who merely takes life. He takes more than that and ruins it, letting his victims live. He's not above killing, oh no, but killing is too fast and final. He likes a longer, more deadly game. How do you ever expect to get him back to Oklahoma?"

Her speech was so vituperative and vehement that for a moment Paul was silent. She was right—Finch had proved himself in the past—but how had she come to see the man so clearly? Of course she could see, because Finch was not only ruining the person closest to her, but also the home she loved and cherished. He was ruining Uriah, too. There must be some way to stop the poison Finch was spreading, some way to destroy the evil he conceived. Tomorrow there must be a showdown.

Paul suggested another, rougher trail down the mountain that led toward the mines and away from Gull Canyon. He thought of a thousand things he wanted to say, but he was afraid that, put into words, none of them would sound right. He wanted to tell her that he'd come back from Oklahoma when everything was settled, but that would sound like an empty promise. Who knew what would happen once he got

Finch back home? It might take months to convict him, and Paul wanted to give no promise that he could not keep.

When they reached the Lone Chance, Norah insisted that he let her go on alone. Knowing why she asked it, afraid that he might see Helen driving home, he did not insist. He started to take her hand but drew back. To touch her would be more than he could bear. He watched her ride away, unhappy and forlorn, until her small, brave body was swallowed by the shadows of the trail.

When Norah left Paul, misery rode with her, misery and helplessness. How could her mother put her in such an unfair position? She was a mature woman, and even though she was still attractive, she must know the difference between infatuation and deep abiding affection. Norah felt her lips tingle when she remembered the kiss Paul had given her back there on the mountain. Why had he become so suddenly amorous? Before yesterday, she would have welcomed his kiss, would have savored the pleasure and fulfillment of it. But now all she could say over and over to herself, was Tomorrow he'll be gone and I'll be free—tomorrow he'll be gone and I'll be free! But deeper down, an echo repeated, Please don't let him go—please don't let him go!

The sun had set when she reached the ranch. She rode to the barn, unsaddled her horse and turned

TWISTED TRAILS 151

him into the pasture. She picked up her saddle and took it inside, where she placed it carefully on the saddle buck, then hung up the bridle. She saw the buggy was missing. It could mean only one thing. Then another thought struck and startled her. When Paul had gone to catch his horse up on the mountain, he could have looked down into Gull Canyon. Had he seen anything? Had he seen the buggy there? Was that why he had come back to kiss her so passionately?

She was about to leave the barn when she heard the rattle and clink of the buggy coming into the yard. So her mother had gone to meet Finch, and now she had come back to exclaim how exhilarating her lone rides were. But when Norah looked out the door, she saw Alonzo Finch helping her mother from the buggy. They were talking seriously, and Finch was smiling as they went into the house.

Norah felt a new pang of anxiety. How did her mother dare to take such a chance as this? Did she care nothing for the feelings of others? Suppose Uriah should happen to come home just then? Knowing what she must do, and furious because she had no alternative, Norah went to the house. Should Uriah come and find the three of them there, he could have no cause for suspicion.

She reached the porch and was about to enter the door when she froze in her tracks. Voices, low and urgent, were audible just inside.

"It came up very suddenly, Helen. I'm sorry," Finch said.

"Alonzo, I don't know what to do," Helen replied, distressed.

"I'll send word tonight or in the morning. You do just as I tell you," Finch said.

Norah, forcing her legs into motion, fled quietly from the porch and disappeared around the corner of the house. After Finch had gone, she hurried into the house to find her mother nervously pacing the floor.

For a moment Norah stood with her back against the door, trying to think of the right thing to say. To blurt out what she had overheard would probably infuriate her mother. She had to take a more roundabout, diplomatic way.

"What's the matter, Mother?" she asked, trying to keep her voice steady.

"Nothing," Helen retorted. "What makes you think anything's the matter?"

"I saw Alonzo riding away. You're upset."

Helen whirled. "Are you spying on me?"

Norah tried to stop the angry shaking of her body. The woman standing before her was a strange woman. The house, its virtue threatened and its dignity gone, was a strange house.

"Others have been spying on you, Mother. Eglund saw you up in Gull Canyon and thought it was I.

TWISTED TRAILS 153

I let him think so. I let Paul think so, too. I was prepared to come into the house if Uriah showed up, to spare him hurt and shame. I can't go on doing such things. When are you going to come to your senses?"

"But you don't understand," Helen pleaded. "It's not the way you think it is."

"How do I think it is?" Norah interposed. "All I know is that I'm being forced to acknowledge lies to spare you gossip and disgrace. I can't go on that way."

"You're a fool, Norah. I was doing all this for you—to give you a chance to get away from here into a world of people and affairs, where life is more than a niggardly scrabble for the bare necessities."

"And to do this thing for me—this thing I loathe and detest—you are willing to compromise yourself with Alonzo? There's no logic or wisdom to your statement," Norah said mercilessly.

"You don't know what a compromise is," Helen said.

"When people see you embrace, what do you call that?"

"You don't take me for a naïve, inhibited schoolgirl, do you? A man like Alonzo needs stimulation to make him do what you want. I think he'll do the right thing when everything is settled. I wouldn't want to stand in your way. . . ."

"Stop it!" Norah cried, stamping her foot. "You're twisting things around to make me take the blame. I've told you Alonzo is no good, and I believe what Paul said about him. I wouldn't go away with him if he were the last man on earth. Now stop trying to excuse your indiscretions by saying they were for my own good!"

Her mother broke down and, sobbing violently, stumbled up the stairs. Norah felt the tension and anger drain out of her, to be replaced with love and forgiveness. How could she judge her mother's needs when she had not had her mother's environment and conditioning? Once Alonzo was gone, and this flurry of excitement past, her mother would realize the value of the security and affection Uriah gave her.

It was growing late, and Uriah would soon be home, so Norah prepared the supper, with Cherry's help. When Uriah arrived, Norah explained that Helen had a bad headache, a difficult lie because Helen was seldom sick. Uriah, concerned, suggested going up to her, but Norah stopped him with the excuse that Helen might be asleep.

Supper was a lonesome meal without the stimulus of her mother's conversation. Norah made several attempts to discuss things, but because the things she wanted most to discuss were impossible, she had little success. Uriah, always an early riser, went to bed

TWISTED TRAILS 155

soon after supper, and Norah and Cherry washed the dishes and cleaned up the kitchen. Even after Cherry retired to her room off the screened porch, Norah remained in the kitchen, waiting for she knew not what. She kept the lamp turned low.

Much later, there was a quiet knock on the kitchen door. Norah opened it cautiously, keeping the lamp behind her so that her face was in total shadow. Eglund spoke through the crack of the door.

"I've got a note here from Finch. He said you expected it, ma'am," Eglund said softly.

"I'll take it," Norah said in a throaty whisper.

Chapter 8

Inside the Lone Chance, Paul looked around. There were several men drinking at the bar, and one card game was in progress. Finch was not there. Eglund was there, sitting to one side and watching the door as he nursed a beer. When he saw Paul, he motioned him over. Paul took a seat on the bench and waited.

"I found them gold pieces of mine on top of my bunk, Paul," Eglund said slowly. "I heard how you was shot at. I reckon that there gold needs some explaining. I didn't shoot at you. I came to tell you who killed Big-head. I've been sellin' booze to the army post and some to the Indians. In fact, it was me who stuck the booze in your hay. Drunk Indians ain't as bad as some sober white men."

Paul listened in silence.

"Crooked-eye, that Indian brave with a cast in his eye," Eglund continued, "is always after me for hooch. He told me today if I'd get him some firewater, he would tell me who killed Big-head. I promised, and he talked. He said he saw Big-head riding out into the valley after dark. He even called to him, but Big-head rode away like he was scared. Then Finch came down the same trail and offered Crooked-eye a bottle of hooch if he'd help find Big-head. An Indian can see in the dark and hear like an elephant. They overtook Big-head. There was an argument about whether Big-head had told you who had hired him to kill you. Finch drove a knife in Big-head's back. Then he had Crooked-eye give him an arrow, and he forced the arrow into the wound. After that he propped Big-head on his horse, so that he wouldn't fall off right away, and turned the horse loose. Crooked-eye said he didn't like the business, so he found two other braves, and they proceeded to get drunk."

There was a little confusion as to timing, but otherwise the story was logical enough. Captain Cranny, the post doctor, couldn't be trusted as to the hour Big-head had been killed.

"Would you and Crooked-eye tell this in court?"

"I reckon so. I just wanted to clear myself with you, Scott."

"Thanks, Eglund. Don't talk to anybody else about it for now, will you?" Then he added. "Come on; I'll buy you a drink."

Before Eglund left, Paul told him, "Bring Crooked-eye here in the morning. I'm going to brace Finch tomorrow if I must. If the warrant doesn't come, I might persuade him to come home with me instead of facing a murder charge here. After all, Oklahoma deserves first chance at him."

Later, when Finch came into the Lone Chance, Paul slipped quietly to his room. He wanted no argument with Finch this night. He doubted he could talk to the man without losing his temper. Tomorrow, in the daylight, would be soon enough. Sitting on the side of his bed, having a last cigarette, he heard light footsteps on the stairs and a knock on his door. He was irritated when his caller turned out to be Gladys.

"Go away," he said wearily.

"I'm not here for myself," she said tartly. "Norah Young is out front. She said to come to the ranch. Sodek is worse."

"I'm sorry I was short with you, Gladys. I apologize," Paul said.

"Let it ride," Gladys said. "I deserved it."

Downstairs, Norah was standing. Asking her to wait, Paul hurried to the corral behind the Lone Chance and got his horse. When they were on the road, he asked:

"Is Aaron much worse?"

"I think he's dying, Paul," she said with a catch in her throat.

"He's a tough one; don't worry."

"But he had that bad lung. The kick in the ribs has made it worse."

"Curse Stebbins!"

"Cursing won't help."

"If he's dying, what does he want with me? Has he no kin—"

She looked away without answering, and he let the matter die. On reaching the ranch, they went directly to the bunkhouse. A lantern burned inside, and Uriah's huge shadow filled the room as he sat near the bed. When Paul entered, Uriah went out without speaking. Paul leaned over the wheezing form on the bunk.

"Aaron, it's me, Scott. Buck up old man; you'll pull through," Paul said.

Aaron mumbled unintelligibly. His shaggy head twisted, and for a moment his eyes shone brightly.

"Good—good boy. You done me a favor an' got yourself beat up for it. I ain't got long to live, Scott. Norah's been like a daughter to me, and I want you to take care of her. She needs a good man before she gets in trouble with the riffraff at the post or the mines. Reach under my pillow, son. There's a paper there. That's it. It's a map showing where my diggings are. They're yours—yours an' Norah's. It will help you take care of her. Now—I guess the Angel Moroni is blowin' his horn for me."

Paul went to the door and called to Norah and her father, but before they returned to the bunk Aaron was dead. Paul stood for a moment, angered and sorry. He had learned to like the old man in the short time he had known him, and it seemed unfair that he should have been the victim of such a tragic bit of horseplay. Stebbins was morally guilty to a certain extent, but what little law was there would never touch him.

"He gave me this paper," Paul said. "It's a map of his diggings, so he said. Wanted me and Norah to have his mine." Paul held the paper under the light of the lantern.

"I know." Uriah nodded. "He never had a mine. That land belongs to the gold mining company on the hill. Farrow knew Sodek was digging on company property, but I made a deal with him. I turned back most of the gold Uriah scrabbled for. The rest, with what money I could spare, I sent at intervals to his family."

"Then he does have kin?" Paul said quickly. "The mine should belong to them."

"The mine already belongs to the company," Uriah repeated. "Aaron was too proud for charity, and his troubles drove him into the hills. He had two wives and families, and when polygamy was banned he had to split them up. Both women was jealous of him, so he couldn't pick one to live with. They danged

TWISTED TRAILS 161

near nagged him to death. He took it to heart, and it broke him. Neither of his wives knew where he was; that's why I sent the money for him. His kids is grown now. They'll get along all right."

"He needs burying," Paul said, while he mulled over Uriah's strange story in his mind.

"Me an' Eglund will tend to it," Uriah said.

When Paul left, Norah whispered goodbye. He had to drive himself hard to leave her standing there while hunger for her lips besieged him. He had no right yet to break the barrier between them completely.

Eating his breakfast the next morning, Paul felt the tension of his sinews and of his mind. Today held forth a promise, deadly or beautiful. His eyes searched for Finch, but Finch was not downstairs yet. Paul finished his coffee and strolled into the bar. The room was empty except for the barkeep, who dozed in an old Wells Fargo chair. Paul slapped his hand on the bar to rouse the man.

"Have you seen Finch this morning?" he asked.

Blinking owlishly, the stout man scowled. "Yeah. He was here early—very early for him."

"Where did he go?"

"I don't know. I ain't no detecatif. Kinda heard a horse cloppin' by toward the north trail."

Puzzled and impatient, Paul went outside. The

still low sun poured its golden light across the land, stirring the shadows in the gullies and slowly chasing them away. There was the smell of dust and sage on the breeze. Paul started for the railroad camp, but Carmody, on his way to the Lone Chance, met him before he got there.

"What's this I hear about Finch leaving early this morning, Scott?" Carmody boomed.

"That's what I wanted to ask you about," Paul countered.

"The flunky over at the cook tent said he saw Finch heading out the north trail just after sunrise. I don't like it," Carmody said.

"Why?"

"Doggone it, Scott, my payroll money is on the road today. That rickety outfit with the old man driving is coming in on the north trail."

"Finch doesn't know that," Paul said. "I figure Finch knows I might get that warrant today, and he's giving me the dodge. I aim to go after him, no matter what."

"You hired out to ride guard on the stage today," Carmody reminded him.

"Okay; I will. I'll ride out the north trail, catch Finch and then cut south until I hit the stage road. I'll pick up the stage and ride in with it," Paul explained.

"How will you manage Finch?"

"I'll have a rope and I'll have a gun," Paul said. "I haven't crossed horns with Finch yet, but I aim to have a try. He'll either have to kill me or come back."

"You want help?"

"There's only one of him," Paul said.

"I like your style, Scott," Carmody said, extending his hand. "Good luck."

Paul went to his room and buckled on his gun. As he went out, the cook looked up and said, "What's eatin' you, pardner?"

"Nothing. If Addie asks for me, tell her I've gone out to do a job."

Paul went to the barn, saddled his horse, mounted and set out at a brisk pace toward the rising sun. He had his rope, his gun, and his hate with him. That was all he needed for his showdown with Finch. The trail angled off along the foothills, diving into gullies, vaulting over the eroded ridges that spread out from the mountains like the fingers of a giant hand. He entered the cedar breaks where the juniper and pinion trees grew so thick they hemmed a man in. On and on he rode, here and there, where the earth was soft or the dust thick, picking out the tracks of the horse with the long, narrow shoe. He had followed that track once before. He hoped to be following it for the last time.

Over and over he debated in his mind what he

would do when he found Finch. If Finch ran, he could rope him. If Finch fired, he could wound him. He had to get Finch back to Camp Boyd. Once he met up with the stage—

Paul pulled up with a jerk and stared with surprise at what he saw on the narrow, rough road ahead of him. Stopped in the bottom of a wide swale was a rickety buckboard, the bony horses standing slack and idle in the road. On the seat of the buckboard the grizzled driver was slumped over, fast asleep. There was humor here, but the humor had a grim undertone of danger. Suppose somebody should get wind of the subterfuge? Certainly no holdup could be more easily accomplished. With growing alarm, Paul noticed that the sleeping driver had a gun hanging limp in one hand. Could he be drunk? Precious good a gun would do him in his present condition. Paul felt a thrust of anger, because he hated to see any man take advantage of his employer or be derelict in his duty. He shrugged and rode forward. Carmody must have known the man he was trusting.

As he drew up alongside the buckboard, Paul knew something was wrong. He dismounted, leaned over the slumped driver and saw a huge splotch of blood on the man's shirt. Here was murder—here was death! Carmody's little scheme had backfired. Paul tried to move the driver from his slumped position and heard the sucking in of air. Quickly he felt for a heartbeat. It was so feeble that it was scarcely noticeable, but it was there.

Finding a canteen of water under the seat of the wagon, Paul splashed some over the driver's grizzled face. The man's head moved, and his eyes flickered open vacantly.

"Take it easy, old-timer," Paul said softly. "Here; let's see if we can straighten you out."

The man mumbled something unintelligible and tried to shake his head. Paul wished for whiskey, but he had none. He held the man's head back and forced water between his parched lips. For a moment the man revived, and Paul managed to turn him around and lay him back on the wide seat.

"What happened?" Paul asked hopefully. In his mind he had already guessed what had happened. Finch had ridden that way, and where Finch was, evil followed. Finch had shot the man, Finch had taken the money—

The man heaved a great sigh, and his eyes opened, clear and sane for a moment. His lips moved.

"Lieth—Lieth Severs. He was riding with me. Caught up with me back a ways. I let him ride— keep company." The man's blood-flecked lips stopped for a moment. With a great effort he tried to speak again. "Lieth Severs tried—tried to shoot—no chance. Went—south. . . ."

The old man's head twisted, and his body appeared to shrink as blood trickled from the corner of his mouth. If Paul had arrived earlier, he might have stopped the bleeding, but it was too late for that. He had to think about what the old man had said. All Paul had been able to get out of the disjointed sentences was that Lieth Severs had caught up with the old man and had been allowed to ride along. Then he had shot the driver, taken the money and headed south. But Finch must have fitted into it some place.

Gently Paul covered the still form on the seat with a tarp he found in the wagon. Then he searched for tracks. Heading away from the wagon were the long, narrow tracks of Finch's horse, and mingled with them were tracks of a different kind. Grimly Paul mounted and followed the trail. The horses had been traveling fast; that was evident by the length of their stride and the depth of the hoof marks. If Lieth Severs and Finch were together in this holdup, why should they be so frantic to get away from the scene of the crime? He realized now why Addie was unhappy.

Paul rode warily. Here was the work of desperate men, and he had been warned and shot at already. If he blundered into an ambush, he would have little chance of surviving. This was wild country, lawless country to a great extent. A lawless country became a sterile country, for no man could settle and grow without the law. Some day things would be

TWISTED TRAILS

different, and those who pioneered would enjoy the fruits of their labors.

He stopped his horse abruptly as the animal threw up his head and snorted. This was the manner of a horse around death. Paul searched the rough, broken landscape. Then, near a ledge of rock, Paul saw the body of the horse. Forcing his mount as near as he could to the dead animal, Paul dismounted and continued curiously on foot. The downed animal was still saddled, and it was not Finch's horse. It must belong to Lieth Severs. Paul walked around the animal, and there he saw the man pinned against the jagged rocks. He lay with his face hidden against the bright heat of the sun. Paul wanted to turn him over, but he had first to make sure it was safe.

He picked up the outflung arm and felt for a pulse. The pulse was strong.

He said loudly, "Can you hear me?"

There was no reply. The man had been thrown hard and evidently knocked unconscious. Then Paul saw the blood under his head and knew he had been shot. Paul had never seen Lieth Severs before, but there was something oddly familiar about the twisted figure. A leg was pinned securely under the fallen horse, and the horse had to be removed. After some coaxing, Paul got his mount near enough so that he could attach his rope to the carcass of the dead horse in such a way as to roll the heavy weight off the unconscious man's leg. When this was accomplished, he went back to the prone figure.

The leg had been horribly mangled across a sharp blade of rock as the weight of the horse crashed upon it. Now it lay in a tangle of bloody cloth, the broken bone exposed. It was a sickening sight, but one to be endured. The lifting of the weight off the leg had started it bleeding again, and Paul had to tie a tourniquet above the break to stop the flow of blood. This accomplished, he dared to turn the man over. He did this as gently as he could, and when the unconscious man was looking up at him, he caught his breath and let out a low curse of surprise. It took a long time for him to accept the truth, for it was totally unexpected. He had heard of Lieth Severs, he had conjured up a picture of him from all the talk, but he had never dreamed of anything like this. The face that looked up at him was that of Larry Scott! Larry Scott, his own brother!

Paul moved in a daze, and he remembered things that now made sense. This was why Finch had come to the valley, because he knew Larry was there. Alonzo was still using Larry, probably under the threat of exposing his past. Here was Larry, broken and ruined, while Finch was still free, his pockets lined with money Larry had almost died to steal.

There was a canteen of water on Larry's saddle, and Paul took it and bathed Larry's face, forcing some of it down his mouth. He washed the blood off the nasty crease alongside Larry's head. Finally Larry opened his eyes. He looked straight up at Paul, and there was defeat in his eyes. But it wasn't total defeat; it was mingled with remorse and defiance.

"Hello, Paul," Larry said quietly.

"How did you ever get mixed up in this, Larry?" Paul asked gently.

"I thought I could start over here," Larry said. "I found Addie, and we would have made it fine if Finch hadn't come. He learned I was here and came to blackmail me. This job was to be part of the blackmail. When I learned you were in the valley, I wanted to pull out of this job, and I told Finch so last night. He wouldn't let me."

"How could you always be so wrong, Larry?" Paul asked sadly. "If you could just once find the strength—"

"I found it today, Paul," Larry said almost in a whisper. "I found it today, and it's too late. I knew about the payroll money and how it was coming in by rattletrap. Carmody's done this before, and Addie and I knew about it. Finch promised to go and let me alone if I'd help him pull this job. I got back from Salt Lake last night and talked with Finch. But I kept out of sight and headed back along this trail. This morning I overtook the buckboard and rode with old Hitchens, the driver. Then all of a sudden I changed my mind. I told Hitchens of the danger, but when Finch came, we couldn't talk him out of it. He shot us both and got the money. I think I wounded Finch, but not bad. I got grooved in the head and was out for a minute, and when I came to, I hightailed it after Finch. He killed my horse and got away with the money."

"We've got to stop Finch, Larry. Can't you see that?"

"I figured if he left the valley you'd go with him, and I could stay here in peace. It's a lovely valley, Paul. But I'm tired, and I'm through. The one good thing I ever tried to do, this thing today, I botched up."

"I've got to get you to town. Then I've got to go after Finch."

"My leg's killing me, Paul. I'll never make it."

"You've got to make it. Addie needs you."

"Addie's too good for me," Larry whispered.

"Put your arms around my neck; I'm going to try to lift you," Paul said.

Larry complied, but as his weight buckled his shattered leg, he moaned and lost consciousness again. By a superhuman effort, Paul managed to get Larry across his back and carry him to his horse. Heaving him across the saddle like a sack of meal, he roped him in place. Then he walked back toward the buckboard, leading the horse with its sad burden.

TWISTED TRAILS 171

When Paul drove the buckboard up to the Lone Chance with its burden of misery and death, it was afternoon, and a few idlers on the porch and some of the men from the railroad camp, who were anxious for their pay, clustered around. Paul saw a man mounted on a horse, and he spoke to him.

"Ride like the wind to the army post, and bring the doctor," he ordered.

As the man took off, Addie came to the door, with Carmody right behind her. Paul dreaded what Addie must see, but there was no way of avoiding it. She came down the steps warily, as though sensing something wrong. Carmody hurried past her.

"What happened, Scott?" he barked, his eyes scowling.

Paul kept secret Lieth Severs' true identity for the time being. He said, "Lieth Severs, on his way back from Salt Lake, was riding with Hitchens in the buckboard. Finch held 'em up and killed Hitchens. He almost killed Lieth. . . ."

Addie said with a catch in her voice, "Is Lieth hurt? Where is he?"

"Here, Addie," Paul said, pulling back the tarpaulin to reveal the dead man and his unconscious partner.

"Lieth!" Addie said as though the word were torn from her. "Oh, Lieth."

"I've sent for the doctor," Paul said. "Get him in

bed, Addie; that's all you can do. Get him in bed and pray. I'm going after Finch."

"Finch?" somebody in the crowd repeated. "Why, I saw him heading up Gull Canyon not an hour ago. I was rabbit hunting in the big gully, and he was riding up that way out of sight most of the time."

"Thanks," Paul said.

"I'll go with you," Carmody offered.

"You stay here and help Addie," Paul told him. "Finch is my meat, remember?"

With that, Paul mounted and turned his horse toward the mountains. He was a little confused and perplexed by the news that Finch had come back so close to the Lone Chance. Did he, believing that Lieth Severs and old Hitchens were both dead, expect to come back to Camp Boyd and deny any knowledge of the holdup? That seemed a little farfetched, yet if what he had just heard was true, Finch was back. Why? He could not expect to keep up a life of crime in such a sparsely settled part of the country without being found out.

Paul crossed the big gully and turned up the road toward the line cabin in Gull Canyon. Gull Canyon led nowhere. Why had Finch gone up there? Of course, the man could have been mistaken, and it might have been somebody else he had seen. Finch was now a murderer with a living witness against him. He had money. Had he come back for some-

TWISTED TRAILS 173

thing else? A woman?

Paul worried that thought as a dog worries a bone. What woman? Guiltily he remembered what he had seen from the hill trail yesterday when he had been riding with Norah. Something must have gone wrong for Finch. That thing must have been Lieth Severs' resistance. If Severs had gone along with the game, they could have killed the old man and spirited away the money. Lieth could have pretended to return from Salt Lake in the day, and Finch could have come back without a witness against him. But Lieth Severs, born Larry Scott, had found his conscience and his courage. And Lieth was still alive.

Paul made a turn in the canyon and pulled swiftly into the tall choke-cherry bushes at the side of the road. He could see the cabin, and before it stood the Young buggy. What crazy scheme had Finch convicted now? Was he planning to lure Helen Young away from her family for pure hate? For revenge against Norah? Certainly Finch could not be true to any one woman for long. How could a woman like Helen become infatuated with him?

Finch's horse was nowhere in sight, and he wondered if Finch had been there and gone. Paul could take no chances, for Finch was now a desperate man, a man who could win freedom only by destroying anything in his path. It was true he might believe Severs dead, in which case he would have time to complete his perfidious scheme.

Keeping in the bushes, Paul dismounted and crept forward on foot. Nearer the cabin, the bushes were scattered and he had to depend upon luck. He felt of his gun and, crouching low, ran the last twenty feet to the door. Drawing his gun, he thrust the door open and stepped inside. For a second he stood shocked speechless, looking at the woman standing in the middle of the room.

"You?" Paul gasped incredulously. "You?"

"You don't understand," Norah said, her voice pleading.

"You were going to leave with him—with a thief and a murderer?" Paul said relentlessly.

"No—no."

"Where is he?"

"His horse was hidden out in back. He took off over the hill. He was wounded in the side. Paul, you've got to stop him."

"Why? Where is he going?"

"Maybe to the ranch."

"Why do you say that? Tell me the truth, Norah. You've been holding back from me, and I want to help you. You can't protect your mother any more. . . ."

"You knew!" Norah gasped.

"I saw the buggy here with Finch's horse tied to it yesterday."

"I see," Norah said resignedly. "All right; Alonzo sent my mother a note last night. I intercepted it. I might as well confess everything. I opened the note and read it. I don't care what you think of me."

"I think you did right, Norah," Paul said quietly, putting his hands on her shoulders. "What was in the note?"

"It told my mother to meet him here today—now. She was to bring something with her, something important, but I don't know what it was. They were going to go away, so the note said. I kept the note. I came here in place of my mother, but Finch cursed when he found me here. He would have struck me, if I hadn't seen you coming up the trail. I tried to get him to go away and leave my mother alone, but he laughed and called me a simple fool who didn't know what life was all about. Even when I promised to go with him, he refused. There was something more important to him than any woman."

Paul said, "Finch doesn't know what a tight spot he's in. He may go back to the Lone Chance. I'm going there first, Norah. You go home and stay there."

Paul saw the distress in her eyes, and his heart swelled for her. Hating Finch, she had offered to sacrifice herself for love of her mother. But the sacrifice had been for naught.

Paul watched her until she got the buggy turned

around; then he set out over the hill on the shorter trail to the Lone Chance. Finch was ahead of him, out of sight, but Finch was no fool. He knew that Paul would stay close on his heels. But if Finch believed that Hitchens and Severs were dead and nobody yet knew of the murder, he might still try to bluff it out, at least until he could get his hands on whatever it was Helen Young had.

Riding out of the big gully, Paul cut directly for the Lone Chance. The idlers on the porch looked at him curiously, and Farrow from the mine met him in the doorway. Farrow's loose, skinny frame stiffened, and his pale face sought Paul's eyes.

"I heard about the ruckus, Scott," Farrow said. "Did you find Finch?"

"Not yet. He got away from me up there, and I thought he might be here."

"It ain't likely he'd come here. I told you I was troubled with highgraders on that rich gold quartz we struck. It appears Finch was back of that, too."

"Everything he touched rotted," Paul said bitterly.

"We were tipped off he had the stuff hidden in the shack in Gull Canyon. We staked some men out there last night and searched the place but found nothing. I reckon he must've caught onto our scheme an' took the gold away, but it ain't in his room. We watched him until this morning, and he got away from us. I figure that's why he came back—to get that gold."

"I wouldn't know, Farrow," Paul said. "I'll handle it, if you want. Where's Addie?"

Farrow jerked his bony head toward the stairs. "Wearin' out the carpet in the hall upstairs," he said.

Paul mounted the stairs, his mind clicking over. It all fitted together. Helen had gone to the line shack yesterday, and Finch had gotten her to take the gold away. Nobody would follow Helen; nobody would suspect her of aiding a thief. She had taken the gold, and was supposed to have returned with it today, but Norah had prevented that. Paul felt a sudden fear because Finch, desperate, might hurt or kill anyone who opposed him.

Paul paused in the upper gloom, and was face to face with Addie. Addie's eyes were bright, her cheeks flushed, and the stain of tears had marred her make-up. Her reserve appeared to have deserted her, and she was only a grieving woman.

"How is he?" Paul asked skeptically.

"He's going to lose his leg above the knee."

"Oh, no!"

"That's all right," Addie said without rancor. "He'll get along. He's got more guts than I thought he had. I'm proud of him, Paul—I love him. I guess I loved him before, but he hadn't proved himself. But then, I'd have gone on loving him, because love needs no proof. It's different now, though; I respect him as well. We're going to do all right, Paul, Lieth and I."

Captain Cranny, the medical officer from the post, came from Addie's fancy room where Lieth lay on the soft silk bed. The doctor looked steady and somewhat grim. Whatever shreds of pride he had left he wore now, like an armor. Here was a case to test his skill.

"Mr. Scott," Cranny said, "Mr. Severs wants to see you, alone. He wants to thank you, I presume. You certainly saved his life by stopping the flow of blood. I'm going down to scrub up. You can talk to him now."

What could he say to Larry Scott, his brother, after the bitter years? Larry had at last become repentant, had found the courage to turn upon Finch and give him the treatment he deserved, but repentance is not always enough to heal deep scars. Still unable to find the right thing to say, Paul entered Addie's room and closed the door. Larry Scott lay upon the satin pillow, staining it with his blood, his face a flushed, feverish mask. But his eyes were sane, and his voice was quiet and compelling.

"Paul, is that you?" he asked without turning his head.

"Yes, Larry."

"No, not Larry—Lieth. Larry is gone, Paul, dead and in the past. Please let me have my way in this.

Promise not to own me as a brother, not to anybody. Larry Scott was a fool, branded and twisted into a man who did not recognize evil even when it was pointed out to him. Lieth Severs was weak, but he had no record of crime, big or small. He found a woman and he found love. Today he had a choice, a choice between going the way Larry Scott had gone and going the honest way. He chose the honest way. Would it be too much to ask to let me be Lieth Severs, at least until I've established my integrity?"

"What about Finch?" Paul asked, undecided as to the best thing to do. "He could name you."

"That's a chance I've got to take. But I believe Finch will leave the country today, or die. Carmody's after him; Farrow's after him. He's beyond needing a trial."

"I'm after him, too," Paul said.

"I'm sick, Paul. I might not live through this amputation. I lost a lot of blood, but the doc says I can't make it without the amputation. That's why I want your promise now. If I die and am buried as Lieth Severs, I'll die as a man with at least one good deed in his record."

"All right, Lieth; I promise," Paul said solemnly. Larry Scott had paid in conscience and loneliness for his crimes. Lieth Severs might be the man to redeem him. Paul took Larry's hand and squeezed it tightly. "You'll pull through all right, Lieth. You're from tough stock."

The doctor came back, his sleeves rolled up and a white apron covering his ample paunch.

"Do you intend to help me?" Dr. Cranny asked.

"You can find others, Doctor," Paul said. "I've got no time to lose."

Addie's voice said evenly, "I'll help, Doctor."

"No, Addie," Lieth said, "send a couple of the men up. They'll have to sit on me."

Addie followed Paul into the hall. "What did he say, Paul? I want to help him so."

"Addie," Paul said, a sympathetic smile on his lips, "time alone can disclose what he said. But he did say that he loves you."

Paul saw Addie's smile and was warmed by it. At last Addie had found someone to love and mother. Paul hurried down the stairs, past the line of curious men at the barn and out into the slanting rays of the sun. The day was not yet over. Mounting his horse, Paul decided to check at the trading post first to see if there was any word of the warrant he was expecting. It was even possible that Finch might be found there.

When Paul reached the post, he found Uriah alone inside the dim adobe building. The sun, coming in through the fort-like windows, made golden stripes across the piles of stock and up the whitewashed wall. Uriah looked up, his hooded eyes brooding, and Paul

TWISTED TRAILS 181

wondered if he were aware of Helen's actions. Uriah, patient and kind to those he loved, could be terrible in revenge upon any who wronged him. There was strength in his powerful frame, a strength awaiting only the command of a slow but dreadful anger.

"Howdy, son," Uriah said gravely. "I heard you had quite a ruckus out on the trail this morning."

"News travels fast," Paul said, wondering if the news of Helen's rendezvous had also traveled fast.

"Bellows, the miner you sent for the doc, stopped by and told me," Uriah explained.

"Have you seen Finch?"

"Never comes here. Is he gone?"

"I don't think so. I'm looking for him."

Paul thought he saw a dark hatred in Uriah's eyes, but he wasn't sure. Uriah might suspect something was wrong, he might even have seen Finch at the ranch, but he could not be sure who it was Finch had come there to see.

"He's killed a man now," Uriah said. "How are you going to get him back to Oklahoma?"

"Did anything come for me? I expected that warrant today."

"There was nothing."

"No word from the marshal at Salt Lake or Provo?"

Uriah shook his head. "Ain't you found that letter yet?"

Paul hesitated, knowing what his denial would imply.

"Could be what you want to know is in that letter," Uriah insisted, avoiding Paul's eyes.

"I haven't found it," Paul said.

"Do you reckon," Uriah said, his lips trembling, "that maybe—Helen—oh, no, she couldn't do a thing like that."

"Look, Uriah," Paul hastened to reassure him, moved by the older man's emotion, "it probably just got lost. Maybe it will turn up."

"You want I should look for it?" Uriah asked, not sparing himself.

"I'll look for it myself," Paul said. "Thanks, Uriah."

Uriah, a revealing brightness in his eyes, said, "The thanks goes to you, son."

Paul took the proffered hand and felt the warmth and power in it. Then he backed out the door, trying not to arouse Uriah's curiosity. He believed he knew where Finch could be found, and for Uriah to be the one to find him would be tragic. Killing Finch could never restore a faith and love once broken. Perhaps that love and faith might yet be saved.

Mounting, Paul rode leisurely until he was out of sight of the store door; then he dug steel to his mount and clattered toward the green oasis of the ranch. That ranch was a symbol, the product of a man's

TWISTED TRAILS 183

work and love and hope. A man had to have someone to believe in him, to share and enjoy the fruits of his dreams and his labor. And Finch strove to destroy all this. If he could use Helen to his own advantage, he would do so. But once that advantage had been achieved and exploited, he would cast her off to her shame and sorrow.

Even as his horse's hooves sprayed dust into the air, pounding their way toward death or disaster, Paul tried to think how he could save Helen Young from herself. He had to see her and talk to her, even though she despised him. He would ask her point-blank for that letter, because what it contained might be enough to stop the evil that Finch disbursed so foully.

Before he reached the ranch gate, he saw the buggy careening and bounding along the road leading down from the hills. He saw Norah bent forward in the seat, urging the racing horses to greater speed. Paul felt a catch in his throat at the sight of her.

"The little fool," he said, "the brave, proud little fool!"

Even though he had taken the cut-off, she had contrived to arrive home before the thing was settled, because he had delayed at Addie's and Uriah's. Now, if there were danger, she would be caught up by it. He cursed softly, feeling uneasy and afraid. Afraid? Of what? Perhaps Finch would not be at the ranch. Perhaps he had been there and gone away. If so, Paul could trail him and have the showdown where nobody would get hurt.

The buggy surged into the ranch while he was still a hundred yards from the gate. By the time he had turned into the yard, he saw Norah scramble out and hurry toward the house. He watched her sure young strength and realized how much he loved her. His heart swelled at the thought of her loyalty and courage. He was so obsessed by the vision of her that he failed to see Finch leap off the porch of the house, his hand pressed against his side. He failed to see Finch's horse hidden by the corner of the wall.

"Paul!" Norah screamed, not slackening her pace. "Watch out!"

The warning and terror in her voice primed him for what was to be. He jerked his head around, at the same time rolling from the saddle and digging his heels into the dust to stop his forward movement. He saw Finch's broadcloth back, the stain of blood, his shiny boots. Finch was heading for the hidden horse.

"Hold it, Finch!" Paul commanded sharply. He tensed, praying that Finch would stop and turn. Finch must die, if he insisted, but not from a bullet in the back. To Paul's relief, Finch stopped near the path on which Norah was approaching the house.

"Stay where you are, Finch," Paul said, moving stiffly. "You played your last chips, and you played them wrong." His eyes were busy taking in everything at once. Norah, shocked and dismayed by the turn of events, stood frozen within an arm's length of Finch.

"I warned you, Paul," Finch said grimly, "that some day you'd get your neck chopped off by sticking it out too far. You still got a cockeyed notion you're taking me back to Oklahoma?"

"Would you rather go back to Oklahoma alive, or stay here dead?" Paul asked, watching Finch's white hand. Paul knew a gun was under that smooth coat, and he knew the gun was fast and deadly.

"Suppose I prefer neither?"

"One of the men you tried to kill this morning is still alive," Paul said evenly.

"So?"

"So you are a murderer. You killed before; you killed Big-head."

"And if I kill you," Finch said grimly, "it will make three." Then he added, "Is that the way you want it?"

Paul, his eyes aching with the intensity of his gaze, saw Finch's swift movement, but he did not read Finch's intention. As Finch snatched for his gun with one hand, his other hand reached out and caught Norah by the arm. Paul drew his own gun with a swift cross motion, but by the time it cleared leather, Finch held the struggling girl before him, and his gun was snarling savagely.

Paul stood paralyzed and helpless. The dramatic swiftness and deadliness of the moment threatened to destroy him. Finch, the cheat, had become Finch the killer. Only by adding murder to murder could Finch remain free. Paul felt one of the bullets rake fire across his ribs. Another caught him in the chest, and he was surprised at the gasping cough that came from his lips. He felt dizzy and confused. He saw Finch's white, contorted face, but he dared not fire.

"Paul—Paul," Norah cried, "shoot!"

Paul felt his knees buckle. He marveled that he felt no pain; just the shock and sound of the bullets. Even the fact that he was going to die failed to impress him. It was all impersonal, something that was happening but that concerned him very little.

"Paul!" Norah screamed the word.

The sound penetrated his brain and jerked him back to reality. He felt the weight of the gun in his hand. Then he saw the blurred action on the porch. Helen, her face pale, rushed into the yard, her skirts swirling about her feet. She held a shotgun in her hand.

"Alonzo, you fiend!" she screamed. "You murderer!"

Finch, startled, twisted toward this new danger, and Norah tore herself free and fell to the ground. Paul felt his gun jerk in his hand, once, twice! He

TWISTED TRAILS

heard a thundering roar. Finch stood there, weaving and bewildered. The gun fell from his slack hand, and a ghost of the old debonair smile came to his lips. His lips moved without sound, as though he might be quoting, *"Et tu, Brute?"* Then he fell quietly, twitched a couple of times and lay still.

Paul was surprised to find himself on his knees, trying to propel himself forward. Then Norah materialized beside him and was helping him toward the house. By a grim effort of will, Paul drew upon his remaining strength. He stopped where Helen was on her knees, weeping uncontrollably.

"I killed him," she sobbed. "I didn't mean to. I found out today what a beast he was, but I didn't mean to kill him."

Paul placed his hand on her shoulder and said slowly, "No, Helen, you didn't kill him. I did. It was my job. But you did save my life."

"Thank heaven for that," Helen said through her sobs.

Then Norah was leading him into the house, forcing him onto the couch. She gave him a drink of brandy, and he felt the fire of it flow through him. The pain was bearable now. Norah stripped off his shirt, his boot, cut open the leg of his pants. Then, somehow, Helen was there with hot water and bandages. Together they stopped the bleeding and made him comfortable.

"It's not so bad," Norah said with sympathy. "The slugs were wild, and there's not much blood. A bone in your leg is splintered, but it will be all right until the doctor gets here."

"I love you, Norah," he said, trying to grin.

He saw the bright tears in her eyes. "But you're going away," she said. Then, without waiting for his answer, she reached over to the table and, picking up a letter, handed it to him. "Finch had it," she said simply.

Helen avoided his eyes. He did not need to ask how Finch had acquired it. Helen spoke as though to herself, but loudly enough for them to hear.

"I was a fool, a blind, unreasonable fool. I started out to cultivate him for Norah's sake, but he knew she could see through him, so he worked on me. Why does a woman my age forget everything good and honest and clean when a man like Alonzo plies her with flattery? But I wouldn't have gone away with him. Pray God that Uriah never suspected. I found out at the last just what Alonzo was. I didn't want to believe it, even though I knew the gold he made me hide for him was stolen. He made me give him that letter. When I heard what was said out in the yard, and when I saw he was willing to sacrifice Norah to save himself, I was convinced of the things about him I tried not to believe, and I knew fury and hate."

"Don't fret about him, Helen," Paul said. "He deserved to die. The pity of it was he suffered so little compared to what he made others suffer."

"Read it," Paul said, handing the letter to Norah. She read:

> *Dear Son: You can give up on Finch. His father, Lucius Finch, died of a stroke. He confessed that he had aided Finch in that robbery you were accused of, because his business was going broke. That was how he was able to keep going when others could not. It was his plan to plant the money on you and get you to the scene of the crime. You can come home any time you want now. Love, Dad and Mother.*

"I'm not going away," Paul said, "and I love you, Norah."

"You're not going away without me," she said, kneeling by the couch. "I've loved you from the first time I saw you."

"This is a growing country," Paul said. "It needs a marshal."

He couldn't say any more, because her lips had taken command of the situation.